WHO WAS HE?

"Oh, hi," the little girl said.

He didn't answer. His eyes looked funny, and he shivered as if he was cold.

She didn't think about being afraid until he was close. Then, when she drew in a breath, he was almost on top of her. She felt a sharp crack on the back of her head and she was down on the rocks looking up at the sky. His big hand squashed her mouth. She couldn't breathe.

He tugged at her shirt and a knife sawed and ripped at her shorts. She felt the air on her nakedness.

He was too strong. The blackness roared in the little girl's head, bigger and bigger. . . .

Who was he? Who would be his next victim? If you were Joyce Gilwood, the mother of a darling and defenseless little girl, the answer would be more important than life and death.

THE GIRLS ARE MISSING

Recommended Reading from SIGNET

- ☐ CARRIE by Stephen King. (#E9544—$2.50)
- ☐ THE DEAD ZONE by Stephen King. (#E9338—$3.50)
- ☐ NIGHT SHIFT by Stephen King. (#E9931—$3.50)
- ☐ SALEM'S LOT by Stephen King. (#E9827—$3.50)
- ☐ THE SHINING by Stephen King. (#E9216—$2.95)
- ☐ THE STAND by Stephen King. (#E9828—$3.95)
- ☐ ONE FLEW OVER THE CUCKOO'S NEST by Ken Kesey. (#E8867—$2.25)
- ☐ THE GRADUATE by Charles Webb. (#W8633—$1.50)
- ☐ SAVAGE RANSOM by David Lippincott. (#E8749—$2.25)*
- ☐ SALT MINE by David Lippincott. (#E9158—$2.25)*
- ☐ TWINS by Bari Wood and Jack Geasland. (#E9886—$3.50)
- ☐ THE KILLING GIFT by Bari Wood. (#E9885—$3.50)
- ☐ SPHINX by Robin Cook. (#E9745—$2.95)
- ☐ COMA by Robin Cook. (#E9756—$2.75)

*Prices slightly higher in Canada

Buy them at your local bookstore or use this convenient coupon for ordering.

THE NEW AMERICAN LIBRARY, INC.,
P.O. Box 999, Bergenfield, New Jersey 07621

Please send me the SIGNET BOOKS I have checked above. I am enclosing
$_____(please add $1.00 to this order to cover postage and handling).
Send check or money order—no cash or C.O.D.'s. Prices and numbers are
subject to change without notice.

Name _____

Address _____

City _____ State _____ Zip Code _____

Allow 4-6 weeks for delivery.

This offer is subject to withdrawal without notice

THE GIRLS
ARE MISSING

Caroline Crane

Ⓢ

A SIGNET BOOK

NEW AMERICAN LIBRARY

TIMES MIRROR

PUBLISHER'S NOTE

This novel is a work of fiction. Names, characters, places, and incidents are either the product of the author's imagination or are used fictitiously, and any resemblance to actual persons, living or dead, events, or locales is entirely coincidental.

NAL BOOKS ARE AVAILABLE AT QUANTITY DISCOUNTS WHEN USED TO PROMOTE PRODUCTS OR SERVICES. FOR INFORMATION PLEASE WRITE TO PREMIUM MARKETING DIVISION, THE NEW AMERICAN LIBRARY, INC., 1633 BROADWAY, NEW YORK, NEW YORK 10019.

Copyright © 1980 by Caroline Crane

All rights reserved. No part of this book may be reproduced in any form without permission in writing from the publisher. For information address Dodd, Mead and Company, 79 Madison Avenue, New York, New York 10016.

This is an authorized reprint of a hardcover edition published by Dodd, Mead and Company.

SIGNET TRADEMARK REG. U.S. PAT. OFF. AND FOREIGN COUNTRIES
REGISTERED TRADEMARK—MARCA REGISTRADA
HECHO EN CHICAGO, U.S.A.

SIGNET, SIGNET CLASSICS, MENTOR, PLUME, MERIDIAN AND NAL BOOKS are published by The New American Library, Inc., 1633 Broadway, New York, New York 10019

First Signet Printing, September, 1981

1 2 3 4 5 6 7 8 9

PRINTED IN THE UNITED STATES OF AMERICA

1

Joyce could feel the hot afternoon pressing in around her as she lay on her bed, half drowsing. Beside her, in his crib, the baby kicked and fretted, his small pink limbs flailing the air.

"Adam, what is it?" She sat up and leaned over the crib. "Why can't you sleep?"

He refused to look at her. Perhaps he couldn't see her yet.

"I've had enough of that," she told him. "You kept me awake half the night."

It was no use trying to rest. Not until he wore himself out. She smoothed her bed and tied back her hair to keep it off her neck. The tendrils around her face were damp. But then, so was her face, and so was her blue gingham shift.

The sun had moved to the western side of the house. Time to close the blinds. She looked out at what, until a week ago, had been a cool, luxuriant lawn. Now the grass was dry. The air seemed heavy and full of grit, just like in the city. The trees stood motionless in a light, hot haze. Beyond the stone wall, the meadow lay baking under white-gold sunshine.

With the blinds closed, the room was plunged into half-light.

"Now we can both sleep," she said, but Adam had other ideas. The small fretful noises crescendoed to bleating cries. She picked him up and walked with him back and forth across the room. The bleats subsided into snuffles. This had gone on all night, too, the fussing, the crying, the walking. And Carl, her husband, had breathed peacefully and heavily through the hours. Carl could probably sleep through Armageddon.

She was annoyed, but could not be angry with the child who felt so tiny and snuggly, his hair as soft as a butterfly's wing against her cheek. It was nine years since she had held a baby. Had Gail felt like this once?

With a pang, she thought: I wasn't even there most of the time.

What a different babyhood Gail had had, growing up in that hole of a basement apartment in the city, with an impractical father, rest his soul. At least he had doted on his little girl.

And now there was Carl, who did not particularly dote on Gail, nor she on him, but that was to be expected. And for Joyce, it was as though she was really married at last, really raising a family, and not in the crowded, dirty city, but the clean, green suburbs.

"Mommy, can we go swimming?"

Gail stood in the bedroom doorway, her long legs bare and skinny below her shorts, her lank blond hair tumbled about her shoulders.

Poor Gail. After all those years of deprivation, her rescue had been short-lived.

"I'm sorry, honey, but the baby has to sleep. I know it's a drag." She ought to have timed it better. Had the baby in the fall, after school started.

"But I want to do something."

"I know. Maybe tomorrow."

If tomorrow were not more of the same, with the baby, the laundry, the endless feedings. She hadn't gotten it down to a routine yet.

"Can I go out?"

"Of course you can."

Downstairs in the kitchen, the telephone rang. They had turned off the bell in the bedroom extension so it would not disturb the baby. Gail answered it and held it out to her mother.

Still cradling Adam, Joyce settled herself against the pillows of the big double bed and took the receiver. A familiar wariness stiffened her when she heard the voice at the other end. It was Carl's ex-wife.

Not that she had any reason to dislike or fear the woman. Carl and Barbara had been divorced for a long time. But there was something intimidating about Barbara, always a faintly sardonic tone, husky and superior-sounding. Was it ever possible, Joyce wondered, to like your husband's ex-wife? Probably the reverse was even less possible.

"Well," Barbara was saying, "I guess it's about that time."

Joyce did not need to ask what time it was. School had let out for the summer, the Fourth of July was over, and it was time for Mary Ellen.

"I guess so," she replied.

"Well, now look. Are you sure it's convenient for you?"

A brief hope. "Why wouldn't it be?"

"I just wondered, because of the baby and all."

Joyce had to admit that Mary Ellen would not make any difference there. It was just a silly emotional thing, wanting to keep her family to herself.

"Of course," she said, "it's no trouble at all. Mary Ellen's really self-sufficient."

"Hah! Maybe for you she is. Are you sure it's okay? Is Carl—does he really want her to come?"

"Why wouldn't he? She's his daughter. Barbara, is something wrong? You sound awfully negative."

Barbara gave an embarrassed laugh. "Actually, if you must know, it's about those girls. That just bothers me."

"What girls?"

"*What* girls! Are you serious? Right there in your hometown. Don't you read the paper? Don't people talk about it?"

"No, I don't read the paper," Joyce said. "I don't have time. Carl brings it home at night, and I—"

"Those two girls who disappeared. One of them just this week. You can't mean—"

"Oh, those." She had heard about them, of course. Cedarville was not a large community. And two of them . . .

"Two of them," Barbara went on. "One you could understand, especially the first one, eighteen, she could have gone anywhere. But the kid this week was only twelve, just Mary Ellen's age."

"Listen, they've looked all over," Joyce said. "If the girls were anywhere around here, they'd have found them. Probably they took off somewhere. Greenwich Village, or something."

"Twelve years old?"

"It happens." She felt irritated, wondering what Barbara expected her to do about it.

"Does Mary Ellen want to come?" she asked.

"Who knows? I guess so. Anything to get away from me." Another embarrassed chuckle. "And it's better for her than being stuck in that apartment with me working all day, and all her friends gone."

"When should we expect her?"

"Well . . ." Barbara hesitated. "How about tomorrow?"

"Do you want me to go and pick her up?"

"Oh, no, no. You have the baby. I can take some time off. Tomorrow, then?"

Friday. A weekday. So she wouldn't have to run into Carl.

Gail waited in the doorway. "Was that Barbara?" Joyce had no time to answer before Gail exploded. "I don't want Mary Ellen! She's a pest, and she never helps, and she leaves her stuff all over—I hate her."

"Honey, she *is* Carl's daughter, and we have this arrangement."

Gail took a quick breath and suppressed it. No doubt she was going to say she hated Carl, too.

"Sweetie, I'm sorry. It's hard on both of us," Joyce said, in case that made any difference to Gail. "I've enough to manage without Mary Ellen, but that's just life." Softening, she added, "I miss last summer." When there had been no Adam, and Mary Ellen had come for only two weeks, and it was the first year in all her adult life that Joyce had not been forced by circumstances to work for a living. It had been the three of them, a real family. They had gone on picnics, hikes, and swimming trips. Even when Carl was at work, she and Gail had had a lot of fun together.

Gail flashed her a quick grin, remembering.

The grin faded. "Mommy, why were you talking about people going somewhere?"

"Oh, you know. It's summer, and kids sometimes run away from home."

"Did you mean those girls in Cedarville?"

Gail was too damn smart. "Yes, Barbara saw something about it in the newspaper."

"About them running away?"

"About them disappearing." She had to be truthful. "Nobody really knows what happened to them."

"Then why did you say they ran away?"

"I think it's the most likely explanation."

Yet maybe it wasn't now that there were two of them. But it had to be.

She yawned, and her eyes felt heavy. "I didn't sleep well last night. Adam kept me up. I think I'll take a little rest." She placed Adam beside her on the bed and readjusted the pillows.

"Then can I go out?" asked Gail.

"I said you could. But, Gail—don't go too far, will you?"

A shadow passed across Gail's face. Because of those girls, perhaps. Gail always did worry too much.

"I won't," she promised.

2

At the foot of the stairs, Gail stopped to put on her sandals. What, she wondered, was "too far"?

Her mother knew about the place. They had discovered it together on a walk in early spring. Probably her mother had forgotten, but Gail remembered. Now that summer vacation had started, she went there nearly every day.

Beside her, the grandfather clock chimed a half hour and then resumed its ponderous ticking. A fly buzzed in the sunshine outside the screen door.

She unlatched the door and stepped out into shimmering heat. Crossing the lawn, she climbed through a break in the stone wall and entered the meadow. Insects hummed in the hot, dry grasses. Beside the path stood a twisted apple tree. In the spring it had been a puff of white blossoms. She pulled at one of its branches to see how the apples were coming along. A bird darted out from among the leaves and flew squawking into the woods.

As she walked on through the meadow, over a low hill in the distance she could see part of a roof. It belonged to Mr. Lattimer. He was an old man with a dirty yellow beard, and he lived by himself. People said he was a hermit. They said the ruins behind his shack were all that remained of an estate his family once owned, but the house was gone, and he had no money, and he was a little bit strange anyway. Once Gail had passed quite close to him on the road when he was walking into town to buy his groceries, and he had smelled bad. Her mother said it was alcohol and an unwashed smell. She said he probably never cleaned his clothes or himself. Gail could believe it, for he always wore the same baggy brown pants and shapeless jacket and they were filthy.

Looking over at the roof, she saw thin smoke rising

from the chimney. On a day like this? He really was crazy. She hoped she would never run into him again.

After another stone wall, the path sloped down through a wood and over a brook. There the air was heavy and full of gnats. The brook flowed slowly, passing through a wide culvert under the path. She dropped a leaf into the water and watched it disappear into the culvert, then come out on the other side and move in sluggish circles.

Beyond the brook, the path rose steeply through a jungle of dead white stalks that crackled when she touched them.

And then she was in an airy forest, where the trees made a high roof. When she looked up at the sky, she could not see the whole sun, only starry speckles of it shining through the leaves.

She left the path and climbed a small hill where the rocks were damp and moss grew on the ground. One of the rocks had a flat, jutting top, like the roof of a cave. Under it, the receding stone was broken into small rectangular surfaces that suggested many floors and rooms.

"It's a fairy palace," her mother had exclaimed when they found it. Then she had been embarrassed. Just a touch of her Celtic grandmother, she told Gail.

"Granny really believed in them. I think it's kind of nice. She was innocent. And sweet."

The next day Gail had gone back to the cave-rock, not out of any belief in fairies, but because of the palace. She had made people for it, and a garden of moss and white pebbles. Finally she shared the secret with her friend Anita Farand. Anita was the kind who might have laughed at her, but didn't. She had joined in happily and made her own contribution to the garden.

Gail straightened the pebbles and removed a fallen leaf. She patted a loose piece of moss back into place. Some of the moss was green, some gray, and some had tiny red flowers. Embedded in a circle of white stones was the curved glass lid of a Mason jar. That was the garden pool. Its fountain was a miniature horse, borrowed by Anita from her sister's collection of glass animals. A sprig of sumac, which they replaced daily, was supposed to be a palm tree. Yesterday's tree drooped, but she had to leave it. She had forgotten to bring a new one. Other than that, the garden was fairly tidy now, and she turned her attention to the people.

The men were tiny forked twigs; the women, small straight sticks in wraparound leaf skirts. The queen wore a more permanent garment made from the lacy veins of a last year's leaf.

She set to work, dressing them with special care for a party that was to be held that night on the roof of the palace. The silence of the forest walled her away from the rest of the world. She had almost forgotten it existed, when from somewhere near the foot of the hill came a nearly voiceless laugh.

Gail crouched over the stick figures, hiding them. The snicker came again. She raised her head.

"I know you're there, Anita. I see you."

Black hair, nearly invisible among the black rocks moved behind a tree. Anita scrambled up the hillside. "I fooled you, didn't I?"

"No, you didn't," Gail replied, although Anita had seen her try to cover the dolls.

"Yes, I did. You were scared."

This was turning out to be one of the times when Gail did not like her. She almost wished she had kept the cave-rock to herself, but Anita was always coming to her house, or calling her on the telephone, and Gail had been hard pressed to explain her long absences.

"Look what I brought." Anita uncurled her hand. In it lay a glass peacock, its tail spread wide and blazing with color, blue and green and touches of red, all somehow encased within the glass. "Another fountain."

Gail did not know what to think. It certainly was magnificent.

"We don't need two fountains," she pointed out, feeling the cave-rock slip farther away from her.

Anita said nothing as she moved the horse aside and squeezed the peacock in next to it.

"Where did you get it?" Gail asked.

"From Denise."

"Did she give it to you?"

Defiantly Anita tossed her long hair. "She always lets me play with her animals."

Gail knew it wasn't true. Anita's sister jealously guarded

her collection. Probably Anita had helped herself to the horse, too. And last spring, after one of her visits, a golden cape with a feathered collar had been missing from Gail's doll wardrobe.

Anita seemed to sense her disapproval. She busied herself with the peacock and the horse, trying to make them both fit into the jar lid. She was not ashamed, Gail knew, but only aware of how Gail felt and waiting for it to blow over.

Finally she abandoned the animals, and asked brightly, "Gail, do you want to know what I saw?"

"What?"

"Over there. On the path."

"What is it?"

"You have to come and see." Anita stood up and brushed off her shorts.

Gail followed her down the side of the hill and along the path to a longer, lower hill with a rocky face.

"There." Anita pointed to a crevice among the rocks. It was filled with dry leaves, sticks, and twigs, a mound that overflowed the crevice as though someone had piled them in.

"It's just some old leaves," Gail said.

"There. Don't you see? Come closer." Anita took her hand. "Now look. Can't you see them? All those flies?"

Yes, she saw them, swarms of flies hovering about the leaves, their green bodies glinting in the filtered sunshine.

"Ugh!" Anita stumbled backward. "Something *stinks*."

At the same moment, Gail smelled it, too. She clamped her hands over her mouth and bolted back to the path.

Anita coughed and gasped, flapped her arms and spun around. "Wow," she said, backing against a tree. "I'm never going near there again."

Gail uncovered her mouth. "Me either."

"Maybe it's shit. Maybe somebody shitted up there."

"No, it smelled like something rotten in the refrigerator."

"I didn't even smell it before, I just saw the flies. I thought it was a fly nest. Gail, let's not tell anybody, okay?"

Gail did not know why they shouldn't, but in a way it seemed right. It was sort of a secret thing, there under the leaves. Something, or someone, had carefully covered it, and they were not supposed to find it.

But the cave-rock was gone. She would never be able to go back to the cave-rock, knowing that thing was there. She would have no place to escape to after Mary Ellen came.

"I don't like it." She kicked at a tree trunk. "I wish it wasn't there."

"Well, it is. What do you want to do now, Gail?"

"I think—" Gail looked at the ground, avoiding the hill where the flies were. "I think I'd better go home now."

"Me, too," Anita decided. "I'm going to your house. And I'm going to stay for a while, and then I'll walk around home by the road."

3

Joyce woke from her nap as voices sounded on the stairs. She recognized Anita's. It was good that Gail had someone to play with during the summer.

Rousing herself, she assembled a load of laundry. On her way to the basement she stopped and looked into the sunporch, where they were playing. Dolls and doll clothes littered the floor. Anita did not notice her, but Gail glanced up with a faint smile.

They really were different, those two. Gail, always thin, still had the matchstick legs and wispy blondness of a child, while Anita, without seeming older, gave an unconscious hint of womanhood to come. It showed in her mannerisms, some probably spontaneous, some acquired, such as the habit of flinging back her hair and then preening it with a long, slow stroke of the hand.

It showed in her easy way of handling adults, and it showed, rather surprisingly, in her legs. From the red shorts to the sockless sneakers, they were long, tanned, and shapely.

Upstairs, Adam woke and demanded to be fed. She sat on her bed to nurse him and paged through a magazine with her free hand.

"How to Cope With Your Child's Fears." It was an article she ought to read sometime. Gail had had some terrible fears after her father's death. Most were gone now, but a few remained. Her questions about those missing girls, for instance.

Gradually Adam dozed off. She returned him to his crib and went downstairs to start dinner.

Anita was seated at the kitchen table, whining into the telephone. "Why can't you come and get me? . . . Then will you tell Daddy to pick me up? . . . No, I don't want

11

to, I'm scared of Mr. Lattimer. . . . So much for you, I'll stay here all night."

Joyce unwrapped a freshly thawed beef fillet and began to slice it. "Why are you scared of Mr. Lattimer?"

"Because he's a pervert and he's ugly. And besides," Anita tossed back her hair, "he's in love with me." She flounced away, immensely pleased with herself.

Joyce was shocked. What if he really had made advances to the girls?

Moments later came the sound of Gail's voice. "No, I know what you'll do. You'll make me walk you all the way, and then I'll have to come home by myself."

"So much for you!" Anita burst back into the kitchen. With a sly smile at Joyce, she called over her shoulder, "I guess you're not my friend anymore."

Gail crept into the kitchen and stood close to her mother.

Anita slammed out through the back door. "Good-bye, Mrs. Gilwood. Your daughter's mean and selfish."

"Good-bye, Anita." Joyce watched the black hair swinging down the driveway. "Now what's the matter with her?"

"I don't know." Gail stared at the floor.

"I heard her asking for a ride home. Did she hurt herself?"

"No . . . Mommy, what does it mean when there are a lot of flies around something?"

"It means something's spoiling. I guess. You know how flies are attracted to garbage."

Of course Gail knew. What a silly question.

"What's the matter, Gail? Where did you see these flies?"

"In the woods."

"It might be a dead animal. A rabbit, or a deer." There were occasionally wild deer, even in Cedarville.

"I couldn't see it. It was covered with leaves."

Mixing her teriyaki sauce, Joyce thought vaguely of dead animals, of how rarely one saw a dead wild animal.

Perhaps Mr. Lattimer had died. But how would he have gotten covered with leaves?

And then she realized that nothing could have gotten covered with leaves unless it had died last autumn before the leaves fell, and by now it would be well beyond the stage of attracting flies.

"Where in the woods?"

Gail said, "You know that place we found when we took a walk, and you said it was a fairy palace?"

"That's what my grandmother would have called it. You mean it was *there*, in my grandmother's fairy palace?"

"No, the next hill. It was in some rocks, in a crack in the rocks. There was just a pile of leaves and all the flies. And it smelled bad. It made me sick."

"I should think so, when it's this hot."

Maybe a dead dog. Maybe someone buried a dog, but didn't really bury it, with a shovel. It's very rocky there.

"Mommy, will you come and see it?"

"No, honey, I can't go out and leave Adam. Why do you want me to see it?"

"Because maybe—" Gail ground her toe into the floor, then fled the kitchen.

Joyce peeled and sliced two cucumbers to marinate in sweetened vinegar. A real Japanese dinner.

The telephone rang. It was Sheila Farand, wondering if her daughter had started home.

"She left a while ago," Joyce said, "by the road. There was something in the woods that bothered them. Gail was just telling me about it."

"What sort of something? Don't tell me that Lattimer's been pestering them again."

Then it was true, what Anita had said about Mr. Lattimer. Or was it simply that Sheila believed her daughter's tales?

"No, it was something in the rocks. They said it was covered with leaves, and had a lot of flies around it, and it smelled bad."

"Did they see what it was?"

"No. Probably a dead animal. Or maybe Mr. Lattimer's been dumping garbage." She grasped the phone with her shoulder and grated a sprinkle of fresh ginger over the cucumber.

"Probably," Sheila agreed. "Okay, thanks, Joyce."

Gail came back into the kitchen. "Who was that on the phone?"

"Anita's mother. What were you starting to tell me?"

"Nothing."

"It was about that thing you saw in the woods. Just tell me why it bothers you so much."

"I'm afraid of it."

She could pretty well guess what Gail thought it was, her phobias being what they were. But there must have been something she noticed, perhaps even subliminally, that made this seem beyond the realm of normal experience.

Joyce looked at the clock. In forty-five minutes, Carl would be home. She could not broil the teriyaki until he arrived. There was rice to cook, but Gail could mind that as well as Adam. She must do this for Gail, to help her exorcise those ghosts of fear. To let her know that she still mattered.

"Okay, where is it?" She could not help a little sigh of annoyance, despite her good intentions.

"Are you going?" Gail's look of gratitude made it almost worthwhile.

Joyce received instructions as to where to find the "thing," and Gail on when to cover the rice.

"Come back soon," Gail called as she left, and Joyce wondered if she was right in leaving her and Adam alone for even half an hour.

But she had promised. Resolutely she stepped through the stone wall into the bright, hot meadow. Far in the distance she could see the roof of Mr. Lattimer's shack. Would he have gone all that way to dump his garbage? Not likely. He kept very much to himself and that included his trash. Most of it he burned. The rest littered his own property but extended not an inch beyond.

She descended to the denseness of the brook and an army of mosquitoes. She had not been this way since April. It was almost eerily dark, with the trees in leaf and the sun past its zenith.

And then she was out in the woods. For a moment she could not remember where the fairy palace was. That first small hill. She climbed up to see it and was amazed at what Gail had done. A little garden with pebbles and moss and even a pool, all neatly arranged. What a creative child she had.

Love and admiration for Gail surged within her. She

must get back to her quickly. Scrambling down the side of the hill, she continued along the path. And there, just as Gail had said, was another rocky hill.

She could not see any flies. Perhaps she was in the wrong place, or they had retired for the evening. The rocks seemed full of crevices. Some had trees growing out of them. Others were filled with moss, and leaves, and—

Yes, leaves. In one place the leaves and twigs were piled up to form a mound. She moved closer. And suddenly she was assaulted by all of it, the flies, the droning, the smell. She backed away, fighting waves of nausea.

After several deep breaths she tried again. Closer this time. She picked up a stick. For a moment she stood contemplating the leaves, then dropped the stick.

Still holding her breath, she hurried back along the path, across the brook and up into the sunny meadow, where she collapsed into the grass.

4

Gail greeted her with astonishment. "Did you go there already?"

"I went," said Joyce. "I just love what you did with that fairy palace. It's probably supposed to be a secret, but I couldn't help looking. Gail, why don't you run upstairs and take a bath now, before dinner?"

"Why? It's still daytime."

"Lots of people take baths in the daytime. It'll cool you off, you're all hot and sticky. And look at your knees."

Gail inched toward the stairs. "A bubble bath?"

"Of course. But not too long, Carl will be home. Do you want me to start it for you?"

Then she would know when Gail was in the tub.

"Why does Carl take so many showers?" Gail asked, following her up the stairs.

"Because he gets hot and sticky, too."

In the muggy summer weather, Carl always seemed to melt. But then, it wasn't easy, that daily trek into New York and back.

When Gail's tub was running, and Gail sitting happily among the bubbles, Joyce went downstairs to the telephone in the kitchen. She looked in the directory, first under "P," then realized she hadn't been thinking. *Cedarville, Village of.*

She dialed the number. It rang twice. A voice answered, "Cedarville police. Chief D'Amico."

"I don't know if this is anything at all," she began. "My daughter and her friend—they were playing in the woods near here—"

"Take your time, ma'am. Where is 'here'?"

"Shadowbrook Road. They were playing in the woods, and they found—something."

She thought she heard a change in his breathing, some alertness. He said nothing.

"They couldn't see what it was," she went on, "but it upset them. I went over there—"

She described the mound of leaves, the flies, the smell. "It must have been an animal. I shouldn't have bothered you."

"Where did you say this was?"

"The woods. Up near the Lattimer place, near Shadowbrook Road. But the more I think about it—"

"We'll check it out, Mrs.—"

"Gilwood. No, really, I'm starting to feel like an idiot."

"Don't worry about that, Mrs. Gilwood. You did right to call us. Can you tell me the exact place?"

"You start from the end of Shadowbrook Road, right near Mr. Lattimer. There's this brook . . ."

She directed him along the brook and onto the path. She did not know what those dead plants were, but he couldn't miss them, the bone-white stalks. She described the hill, the second one, the crevice of leaves and sticks. He asked for her full name, her address, and said, "Thanks a lot, Mrs. Gilwood, We'll check it out."

Probably just an animal, she thought again. A dead animal that somebody covered with leaves.

Her ears caught the sound of a car in the driveway. She got up from her chair and lit the broiler.

Carl came into the kitchen utterly wilted, his tie loosened, jacket over his arm. He was a big man, broad-shouldered, with golden brown hair that looked blond in the light. His face was strong and his jaw square. She liked that jaw. Although nature had not endowed him with the outrageous beauty of Larry, her first husband, Carl had an air of calm strength, as though he could cope with anything. And he certainly managed better than Larry ever had at living in the real world.

She kissed his cheek. "Hi, honey. Gail's in the tub, I'll get her out. I bet you'll be glad to see the end of summer."

"Don't talk about the end," he groaned. "This is only the beginning."

"Oh, well, it won't last forever." She ran upstairs and banged on the bathroom door.

"Time's up, luv, there's a line forming."

Gail said something indistinct and petulant. She knew the "line" meant Carl.

While he showered, Joyce quick-broiled the meat. When he came down ten minutes later, she was putting the finishing touches on the table.

He said, "I thought Gail was supposed to do that."

"I made her take a bath," Joyce explained. "I guess she's still dressing. They were playing out in the woods, she and Anita. Got kind of grubby."

"Who?" he asked absently. "Oh, that little sexpot."

"Carl, for God's sake! The kid's only nine years old."

He shrugged and went into the kitchen, where she heard him breaking open a tray of ice cubes.

Sexpot. How could he? And yet she understood what he meant. She had seen it herself that afternoon. A few more years and Anita would be leaving Gail far behind.

Carl came into the living room, an old-fashioned glass tinkling in his hand. He settled back on the sofa. "What sort of day did you have?"

"Hot," she answered.

"Restful? Peaceful?"

"Well—Barbara called. Mary Ellen's coming tomorrow."

He set his glass on the floor. "No kidding. Why tomorrow?"

"I suppose so Barbara won't have to see you. And vice versa."

A mirthless chuckle. "That Barbara. Poor girl."

"She strikes me as more of a woman than a girl," Joyce said. "But I suppose you knew her when she was younger." She went to the foot of the stairs and called Gail.

Carl brought his drink to the table. "So except for Barbara, it was a pretty good day."

"Pretty good, as days go." It was not only Gail's approach down the stairs that stopped her from telling him about the mound of leaves and her phone call to the police. By now, the whole thing seemed too trivial for words.

"How about your day?" she asked as she passed him his plate. She enjoyed hearing about the office. It was where they had met, when she changed jobs after Larry's death. Carl had been a young executive, charming and personable. And pursued. Joyce, so recently widowed, had paid little attention to him, which was probably what piqued his interest.

He grinned, giving a small laugh. "Well, now, you know that place. Does anything ever happen? Same old accounts, same old people, same grind."

"So tell me about the people. Who's doing what? Who got fired, retired, married?"

He pondered the question. "Nobody."

She was hardly surprised, not by the lack of activity, but by Carl's lack of interest. He had never been really people-oriented, and did not much care about any of his colleagues on a personal basis.

"I guess I'll just have to go and visit sometime," she said.

"Why don't you? We can have lunch."

"I was thinking of bringing Adam, to show him off. How would he behave in a restaurant?"

"Don't bring Adam. They've all seen babies before."

She was stung, but had to admit he was probably right.

Long after dinner, when Gail had finished clearing the table and taken her accustomed place before the television set, and Joyce was wiping the last of the kitchen counters, the telephone rang.

A male voice asked, "Is this Mrs. Gilwood? Police Chief D'Amico. You called us a couple of hours ago."

"Yes. Right."

"We checked the place you told us about. I thought you'd want to know."

She listened vainly for a note of humor. A report on Mr. Lattimer's garbage, perhaps. But he was saying, "You were right to call us, ma'am. It's bad news. We can't establish identity yet, but there have been a couple of missing persons—"

"No!"

"I'm afraid so. You say your daughter was upset by it. How much did she actually see?"

"I don't know. Nothing. I don't know what bothered her."

"Does she go out there often?"

"Pretty often." Oh, God.

"Did she ever mention seeing anybody?"

"Nobody except—Mr. Lattimer."

"Okay. Thanks, ma'am."

She hung up the phone and discovered Carl in the kitchen doorway.

"What was that all about?" he asked.

"Oh, Carl, I—" She sat down weakly in one of the dinette chairs. "This afternoon, they—Gail and Anita—they were playing in the woods."

"You told me. And?"

"They saw—I just don't believe it."

"A UFO," he suggested.

"It's not funny. I went over, too. It looked like—a pile of leaves. There were a lot of flies around. I don't know how the girls knew. It frightened them. I called the police."

"Because of a pile of leaves?"

"But, Carl, it *was*."

"Was what? You're a very poor storyteller. You leave out the best part."

"*Not* the best. It's not a story, it's real. Somebody was killed and buried, practically in our back yard."

At last she saw the twinkle disappear from his face.

"Killed?" he said. "How do you know that?"

"People just don't bury themselves."

"It could be any number of things. Could be, for instance, somebody died from an overdose. Not anyone's fault, necessarily, but a lot of people don't like to get involved with that."

"All right," she conceded, "but it's the same thing. A death that someone tried to hide. And *right here*."

"Why the hell," he exploded, "didn't you tell me about this?"

"Because I—after I called them, I decided it couldn't be anything."

"You should have told me."

He thought he was protecting her. They could have faced it together.

"But what if it turned out to be nothing?" she said.

Another outburst. "Are you crazy, letting your kid play there?"

"In the woods? That's what we came to the country for."

"Don't ever let her go there again."

The woods that Gail loved. Her fairy palace, with the beautiful garden.

But Gail wouldn't want to.

"No," she said, "not after this."

And thought, Whoever did it was out there. He could have been watching her.

5

Carl left at seven-thirty as usual the next morning. After another cup of coffee, Joyce set about her chores, clearing away the breakfast dishes and tidying the living room, which always seemed to get untidied by itself. Later, as a welcoming gesture, she and Gail made up Mary Ellen's bed.

Gail worked slowly, mooning out of the window at the driveway. A flash of something caught her eye. "Here they come."

Joyce had debated letting it all slip out, but at the last minute said, "Honey, you won't mention anything about yesterday. You know, in the woods, will you?"

"I wasn't going to," Gail answered in a tone that implied she wasn't going to talk to them at all if she could help it.

Joyce went out alone to meet them.

"Hello, hello," Barbara called, swinging her long legs from the car. "How do you like this weather? I thought we were going to have a nice cool summer, the way it started."

Mary Ellen groaned, "Oh, Mom, you're always complaining."

"Which is something you *never* do," retorted Barbara.

"It's nice to see you, Mary Ellen," Joyce lied. "We missed you last month." Because of Adam's being so new, Barbara had suggested that Mary Ellen skip her June visit.

The trunk was unlocked and out came two suitcases, a shopping bag filled with shoes, a grocery carton of books, records, tapes, and miscellany, including a small red radio.

"Do I get my same room?" asked Mary Ellen.

"Yes, it hasn't changed a bit." Joyce picked up what she

22

could carry. "We're keeping Adam in our room for now anyway. It makes it easier, getting up at night."

"Am I glad I'm finished with that part of it," Barbara gloated.

When all the luggage had been taken upstairs, Mary Ellen asked, "Can I see the baby?"

Joyce led them, tiptoeing, into the room where Adam slept. Barbara stood some distance from the crib and gazed at its occupant with a wry half-smile. Mary Ellen leaned into it, her face almost touching the baby's. He stirred in his sleep.

"When he wakes up," she whispered, "can I hold him?"

Joyce nodded, and watched her reach out a finger to stroke his soft hair.

She was actually a very attractive girl, petite and delicate, unlike her long, rangy mother and her large, tall father. She had none of the awkwardness of most twelve-year-olds, but instead was a little pearl with creamy skin, fine dark hair, and an enchanting aura of young girl mixed with sly, teasing womanhood.

Something like Anita. Yet for all their surface charm, Anita was bratty and Mary Ellen self-centered and rude. Except when she chose not to be.

They tiptoed out of the room and Mary Ellen began unpacking. Barbara stood watching her for a moment, ignored. Joyce said, "How about a cup of coffee for the road?" She had to offer, but still felt awkward in Barbara's presence. They had met only briefly at other times.

"I'd really like something cold," Barbara ventured.

Mary Ellen said loudly, "No alcohol."

Barbara rolled her eyes. Joyce suggested, "Iced tea okay?"

She settled Barbara in the sunporch and served a tray of iced tea and vanilla wafers.

"You've really got a nice place here," Barbara said, looking out at the green lawn, the strip of woodland next to it where daffodils bloomed in the springtime, and the meadow beyond the stone wall. "It's so private. Except I think I'd get a little nervous. I like to hear the neighbors crashing around. It lets you know that people are there."

"I guess I had enough of that before," Joyce said, and scurried to find an ashtray as Barbara took out a pack of cigarettes. Her face must have changed color, she thought, and Barbara could read on it a history of recent events.

"Before what? Before Carl?" Barbara's voice was muffled as she gripped a cigarette between her lips.

"Mmm. Too many neighbors."

"You make it sound like a real tenement."

Joyce flinched, and answered solidly, "It was."

"That was after you were widowed."

If only she could agree. But either way, it would sound as though she had grasped at Carl.

"No, before. You see, my husband was an actor. A hopeful actor. He was still hoping when he died. I don't mean," she went on hastily, "that all actors have to live that way, especially when they have a family, but Larry was very idealistic."

"Idealistic? And he kept you in a place like that?" Barbara blew smoke across the room.

"Idealistic about his career," Joyce explained. "He didn't want to dilute himself by working at something else, just to make a little money. Most actors live, you know, by working at something else. Until they really make it, but that's pretty rare. It's just too competitive."

"Then, uh—who brought in the bacon?" Barbara seemed flustered by her own nosiness, but had to ask.

"I did. Actually, it made sense. I didn't have this other thing, the way he did. And he kept hoping . . . He was so sure . . . 'Just give it a little more time,' he kept saying. And then he died, and it was all over. He never did live to see it get better."

"But it might have," Barbara said. "It might have gotten better."

"Maybe." Joyce stared into her glass at the melting ice cubes and the fresh mint from her garden. "But there was Gail growing up in poverty while he chased rainbows."

"Where is Gail? I haven't seen her. Isn't she here?"

"I have no idea." Joyce realized that she had not seen Gail, either. Not since the car came up the driveway.

Barbara said, "Excuse me for asking, but—what happened? About your husband. Was it an accident?"

"It certainly was not an accident. He was mugged."

"Mugged?"

"He was coming home late at night." *Very late at night,*

the way he always did. Much later than you have to for the theater. "And he was robbed and stabbed in a subway station. And now you can see why I was so glad to get out of the city, and why I love—" She choked back the rest of what she was going to say, for violence had come here, too.

"Anyway," she concluded, "this time, my life seems normal. The way it should be."

Barbara's mouth twisted in a humorless smile. "Good for you."

Still bitter? Joyce sat back and watched her grind out her cigarette.

"However," Barbara added, "I think that's something we'd better not discuss. Although I'd love to."

"I'm sure."

"Oh, well. How do he and Gail get along?"

"Just fine." If you could call it that. Most of the time they seemed to exist on parallel planes. "Why? How should they get along?"

"I just wondered." Barbara took out her cigarette pack, shook one loose, and stared at it.

She said, "You seem like a nice, level-headed young woman."

"I suppose I am. Are you trying to tell me something, Barbara?"

"Yes and no. After all, you've been married, what, a year now? Long enough to get acquainted. Maybe things are different for you."

It was almost funny, Barbara trying to spill out her resentment about him. Naturally an ex-wife would feel that way. She might even try to poison the second wife's attitude.

"I think," said Joyce, "that's a rather loaded subject for us to be talking about."

"Yes, that's what I thought." Barbara sounded relieved. "I did try to stop myself."

Not very hard, it had seemed.

"Well, I'd better be going. You make excellent iced tea, I love the mint." She rose from her chair. Joyce rose, too, and Barbara still loomed over her. She could have been quite formidable, in her tall, worldly way, but she was softened by a streak of warmth.

"I *am* sorry, Joyce. I suppose when a marriage breaks up, there are bound to be reasons. Except I thought they were a little more—integral. I don't know what I'm saying. Anyway, it was just a feeling I had."

"I don't know what you're saying, either." Joyce followed her to the foot of the stairs as she went up to say good-bye to Mary Ellen.

A few minutes later Barbara returned, ready to leave. "I hate to tell you this, but that lovely room is now a shambles."

"Again?" Joyce managed a smile.

"Don't tell me it's a habit here, too. Oh, good heavens, and you keep such a neat house. I know Carl likes things neat. Well, I told her to pick it all up. Just keep after her, will you?"

"I'll try."

"It's adolescence. I was terrible at twelve. Have a wonderful summer, all of you."

Joyce went outside to see her off. Mary Ellen did not appear, but when the engine started, she waved from an upstairs window.

As soon as the car had gone, a shower of pebbles fell from the bank above the driveway and Gail came scrambling down through the rock garden.

"Where on earth were you?" Joyce asked. "It would have been polite if you'd said hello to Barbara. She asked about you."

Gail mumbled something and started into the house. At the door she turned, holding her nose. The whole house smelled of cigarettes. Joyce emptied the ashtray, and washed and dried it. Carl disliked dirty ashtrays. He said they looked obscene. And if it was worth noting that Joyce "kept such a neat house," probably that meant Barbara did not. It must have been one hell of a marriage.

She was putting the tea glasses into the dishwasher when Anita appeared at the kitchen door.

"Hi, Mrs. Gilwood. Can I play with Gail?"

"You didn't come through the woods, did you?" Joyce asked.

"No, I came by the road. Hi, Gail, I'm not mad at you anymore."

Gail did not look pleased, but led the visitor up to her

room, where no doubt the dolls and their paraphernalia would be out all over the place.

Better here than in the woods, Joyce thought as she went upstairs to take care of Adam. How close it might have been, the two of them there alone. What would she do if something happened to Gail? What *did* people do? There had been Larry, and that was bad enough, but to lose a child . . .

She was in her bedroom, nursing the baby, when Mary Ellen knocked at the door.

"Joyce, there's a policeman downstairs. He wants to talk to you."

"Oh—" Joyce removed the baby from her breast. He let out a thin cry of protest.

"Shall I tell him to come back later?" Mary Ellen asked.

"No, we might as well get it over with. What does he want?"

"Just to ask some questions. Anita said somebody got murdered, is that true?"

"Yes. I should have told your mother. I didn't want to alarm her."

She slipped a pacifier into the baby's mouth and carried him downstairs. Mary Ellen had installed the policeman on the living room sofa. He was a powerful-looking man, perhaps in his late thirties or early forties. His eyes were dark, his black hair flecked with gray, and his nose seemed slightly flattened, as though it might have been broken once.

He stood up as she entered the room. "Mrs. Gilwood? Police Chief D'Amico." He held out an identification. She studied it carefully. It could have been a trick.

"You're the one I talked to on the phone last night," she said.

"That's right. I'm sorry to bother you, Mrs. Gilwood. Just a few questions." He edged back toward the sofa, but did not sit down until she did.

"This won't take long," he explained. "We only want to get some idea of who's been in the area. Do you recall seeing anybody, any strangers around here, anybody who doesn't live in the neighborhood or have business here?"

"No, I don't." She tried to think. "I don't see too many people at all. It's a kind of secluded house."

She glanced at the picture window. A secluded house, and at the same time, a fishbowl, with all those windows.

"And a long driveway," she added. "We can't even see the road."

"That's why I thought you might have been aware of somebody passing through here. We can't tell which way they came, but they'd have had to be on foot, going into the woods."

Had someone walked right past this house—to his doom? Or someone, perhaps, at gunpoint. Or—

"No," she repeated, "I haven't seen anybody."

"You said your daughter goes there quite often."

"I guess so. But not now. She wouldn't— Do you mean it was there—how long?"

"Not too long, probably. We think it was kept somewhere else, and we'd like to know where. Someplace cool, it looks like. A cave, or something. We think it was only recently dumped in those rocks. Somebody might have reconnoitered there first, or gone back to look. They'll do that sometimes."

"How could anybody look at it? How could they *carry* it—like that?"

"It's hard to tell about people," he said.

"It would have to be someone who's a little bit crazy, wouldn't it?"

He only smiled. "If you see anybody, or remember seeing anybody, would you let us know? Anyone who seems to be hanging around, or walking in the woods, or doing anything different than usual."

"I will." But there had been no one. She would have noticed somebody near her house.

"Do you mind if I talk to your daughter?" he asked, "since she was out there? The same kind of question."

"I'd rather she didn't—" But there was no way to protect her. Anita already knew, and undoubtedly had talked about it.

She called the girls downstairs, and hovered without seeming to listen, so Gail would be reassured but not inhibited.

"We never saw anybody," Gail declared. "Only Mr. Lattimer, but he lives there. Sometimes he walks around in the woods."

"Who was the dead person?" asked Anita.

"Can't tell yet," D'Amico replied. "We're checking that out."

Anita bounced on the sofa. "Was it one of those people who disappeared?" Her eyes glinted. "I hope it's one of those people. And *I* found him. Her."

Gail asked, "Is it gone now?"

"Since last night," he said, "but I'd stay away from there till we find out more about this."

He thanked them for their help. Gail protested that they had not been very helpful.

"You gave me information," he said. "You told me you didn't see anybody. That's part of it." He turned to Joyce. "Thanks a lot, Mrs. Gilwood. We'll be around. That won't surprise you, will it?"

"It will be very reassuring." She stood at the kitchen door, with Adam fidgeting in her arms, and watched him leave.

Gail came up beside her. Joyce said, "It's too bad about the woods. But you still have the lawn and the garden. At least we have an outdoors, not like in the city."

"I liked the city," Gail replied, her face becoming closed and stubborn.

Because she identified it with her father, while Cedarville meant Carl. And now death.

6

After lunch, while Gail and Anita cleared the table, Mary Ellen remained in her chair, gazing through the picture window. Only at a sound from Adam, upstairs, did she stir.

"Can I help you take care of the baby?"

"Of course," said Joyce, "but I breast-feed him, so there's not much you can do about that."

Inadvertently her eyes dropped to Mary Ellen's bosom, and noticed the swelling. So she was there already. No wonder Barbara had worried about her.

Mary Ellen received a lesson in diaper-changing, then retired to her room. Through its nearly closed door came the tinny strains of the small red radio. Adam was fed and had just been put back in his crib when the doorbell rang.

Joyce wondered, as she went to answer it, whether a killer would bother to ring.

Sheila Farand stood on the doorstep, her black hair straggling loose from its summer bun, her body lean and tan in khaki shorts and a red halter. Beside her was Pamela Cheskill, the exact opposite, a cool blonde in a stylish pale green pantsuit.

Sheila burst out, "My God, Joyce, remember that thing you were telling me about last night? I didn't even think about it, but you know what—"

"Yes, I know," said Joyce as she held open the door. "I went over and looked. And the police were here."

"You what?" Pam exclaimed.

"I went over and looked. That's a beautiful outfit, Pam. Would anybody care for some iced tea?"

Sheila gasped. "I couldn't swallow right now. I keep hoping I'll wake up from this. You went over and *looked?*"

"Not at—it." Joyce steered them toward the sunporch. "I just went over and saw what the girls saw. Gail wanted me to. And then I called the police."

"Oh, you were the one." Sheila sank into a cushioned rattan chair. "They said some woman called. I have a cousin on the force, Herb Mackey, he came over and asked if we'd seen anybody hanging around. I tried to keep it from Anita, but she heard the older girls talking, and then she started bragging that she was the one who saw it first and showed it to Gail."

"Yes, that's what Gail said."

"I'd just like to know what she saw."

Joyce described what Anita had probably seen. "You couldn't really tell. It was just a feeling you got, maybe from the smell. Wouldn't you really like something to drink?"

Pam said, "I'd love something to drink, if you really mean drink. I could use it right now."

Joyce mixed three gins and tonic and returned to the sunporch. Sheila asked, "But how did you know to report it? How did it enter your mind that it was, you know, human?"

"I don't know. I guess after I went there it just seemed too deliberate. But I felt awfully silly."

"You shouldn't have. If Anita'd said anything to me, I might have called them myself. But she didn't, so I thought it was nothing, till Herb came by. I'm telling you, I nearly went into shock. Can you imagine?"

She paused to take a long swallow of her drink, then burst out, "My God, it makes me sick! I'm glad it was covered up and they couldn't see. Do you want to know what Herb said? It was pretty far gone, but he said, even without an autopsy, they— Well, anyway, it was tied up, at least the hands. And there were stab wounds all over, and the worst part—" She drew a line from her rib cage almost to the pubic mound. "He just sliced her open, right down the middle."

"Sheila . . ." Pam set down her drink and clutched at her stomach.

"All cut to pieces," Sheila went on. "She was *gutted*. At least they assume it's a she. I mean, things like that don't happen to men, they're the ones who do things like that. They compared it to Jack the Ripper."

"Sheila, please."

"Oh, I'm sorry, Joyce. Anyway, at least he didn't do it right there. It makes me feel a little better about the girls."

I don't see how, thought Joyce. "That's what they told me, too. It was moved. In that condition. Who'd have the stomach to do that?"

"Listen, honey, the guy must be totally out of it. All that mutilation, how sick can you get?"

"It's making me awfully sick," said Pam. "Mind if I go out and look at your rock garden, Joyce? I saw a beautiful aquilegia, and I just love them. When my Brucie was small, he used to bite off those little round things on the crown so he could taste the nectar."

"It's not much of a garden, I'm afraid," Joyce apologized. "I haven't had time, with the baby."

As Pam's sandals clicked away toward the kitchen, Sheila moved her chair closer to Joyce.

"I wish they'd just lock up that Lattimer and have done with it." She stopped and listened, and in the distance, the back door closed. "It was Lattimer, of course. He's the nut around here. Anybody can figure that out, except they have these technicalities, so they can't arrest him. But now wait, obviously I couldn't say this in front of her, but do you know that Bruce—the husband, not the kid—do you know he has this reputation with babysitters— Just the other night he was driving one home, and he was a little high, and before the girl knew it, they parked on one of those back roads—"

"You're saying that about Bruce Cheskill?"

"I don't know if Pam even knows. Well, to make a long story short, the girl got away, but my God, how can I tell Pam why I won't let June or Denise sit for her anymore?"

"Oh, you couldn't." Joyce sat back in her chair. "You know, I can almost believe it. He's one of those big, beefy types." She tried to think of a word. Sensual? "And he does get slobbery when he's drunk."

"All libido and no brains."

That was the word. Libido. But Bruce did have enough brains to be an advertising executive, which she supposed was fairly responsible.

"Now Mr. Lattimer," she said, "he's so pickled all the time, I doubt if he has any libido."

"Don't you believe it."

"And he's no spring chicken. But maybe, with men, that doesn't make any difference."

"Not with freaks." Sheila rose stiffly to her feet. "I wish they could keep them both under surveillance. What a thing for our poor little police force. Hey, I've got to run. I don't want to leave my kids alone too long."

She collected Anita, plucked Pam out of the rock garden, and drove away. Joyce looked up at the aquilegia in its pocket of stone. Poor gentle Pam, with her love of flowers.

But it couldn't have been Bruce. Even drunk, he would not be psychotic. And Lattimer seemed a mild soul, but you never could tell.

They would arrest him soon. Or someone. They'd have to.

Clearing the dirty glasses from the sunporch, she tried not to think of what Sheila had told her. A torture death, savage and sexual. But for the grace of God, it might have been her own child.

The thought of it made her ill. On her next trip upstairs she could not help checking, and feeling a deep, joyful satisfaction that they were safe. Adam slept soundly. Gail, in her room, was carefully stowing the dolls in their wardrobe case, clearing up from the havoc wreaked by Anita.

Mary Ellen lay prone on the rug in her own room, apparently writing a letter, while she radio fuzzed and crackled on the dresser, playing two stations at once. Clothes were scattered everywhere, on the bed, the dresser, the doorknob. Mixed with them were fan magazines, record albums, and spilled bath powder.

"Mary Ellen," Joyce suggested, "why don't you hang up your clothes so they don't get wrinkled?"

Mary Ellen tossed her a scornful look. "I don't care if they get wrinkled."

"Well, okay, but your mother asked you to try and keep things tidy."

Mary Ellen muttered something that might have been an obscenity, and turned back to her letter. Joyce watched her for a moment, half expecting an apology or an explanation, but there was nothing. Slowly she withdrew. It had never been like this before. Mary Ellen had been sloppy, and at times impertinent, but never downright rude. Never—impossible.

She tried to remind herself of the part of Mary Ellen that was Carl, not Barbara. Of the disrupted life the girl had led.

I won't confront her again, she decided. I'll let him deal with it.

When Carl came home, dinner was far from ready. He seemed in a buoyant mood and did not mind. "I'll have my shower and a drink," he said, opening his briefcase. "Did you see this?"

It was the afternoon *Post.* He folded back the pages. She caught a glimpse of a small headline, the words "Body" and "W'chstr," meaning Westchester County.

"I saw it in person," she reminded him, "and I'm sick of it."

"You told me you didn't see anything. Just some leaves. They said it was like Jack the Ripper. He tore out all her in—"

"Carl, stop it! I really mean that. I'm sick."

He did stop then, and studied her. "Poor girl." Just as he used to say when she had morning sickness.

At least he cared. Larry had always told her it was all in her mind. Briefly she rested her head against his shoulder while he patted her back.

"Mary Ellen's here," she said, withdrawing. "Don't you want to see her?"

His whole face changed—oddly, she thought, taking on a frown of uneasiness. "How is she?"

"Just fine. Got stuff all over her room, been playing her radio all day."

"Is she behaving herself?"

"Well—Barbara told her to clean up the room, and when I reminded her, she got kind of sassy. I guess I should expect it. It must be lonely for her, being shunted around like this."

"What did she do?"

"Oh, just sassy." Perhaps she shouldn't have mentioned

it. It might not have been an obscenity that Mary Ellen muttered, but it had certainly sounded like one.

Carl started up the stairs. Barely a minute later, Mary Ellen's voice came shrilly from her room. "I *didn't* get fresh with her. Look, Daddy, I'm supposed to be on vacation. What do you want me to do, spend my whole summer being a slave?"

Oh, damn, thought Joyce. Carl could be such a bulldozer at times. And why bring it up the very first thing?

Through the general ruckus came a thin, rising wail. She hurried up the stairs.

"Listen, Carl, you asked if Mary Ellen was behaving and I said she got a little sassy, but it wasn't worth all this. And you just woke the baby."

He turned and glared at her. "Would you stay out of it, please?"

She looked past him, into the room. "I'm sorry, Mary Ellen. I guess I felt harassed, and you were a tiny bit fresh, but let's all start over. Carl, hurry up and change. Dinner's almost ready."

Carl whipped off his tie and stalked away to their bedroom, noisily opening and closing the door, letting Adam's screams escape like angry hornets.

Mary Ellen curled up on the bed and resumed whatever she was writing.

Joyce stood in the doorway. "I'm sorry he came at you like that, honey, but you know, I wouldn't talk to you the way you did to me. I think we've both got to learn to respect each other."

Mary Ellen did not reply. Joyce went on, "Anyway, you were right about its being your vacation. We'll make it a nice one. We'll go swimming, take picnics, do all sorts of things. But this isn't a resort with paid help, so we all have to pitch in sometimes. And even in a resort, you'd keep your clothes off the floor, wouldn't you?"

Finally Mary Ellen looked up. "What's this thing you people have about clothes on the floor? It's weird."

"You know how your father is. He's a very orderly person." Joyce abandoned any further attempt at discussion and went to the bedroom, where Carl had stripped for his shower. He was tying on a bathrobe. She picked up Adam, who immediately lapsed into choking snuffles.

"I'm sorry, Carl. I'm sorry I brought it up to start with. It doesn't really matter, it's only a room. Teenagers are like that."

"She's not a teenager."

"Twelve? It's teenage. I was, I remember. She just wants to prove that she exists."

"Little bitch," he muttered.

"Carl!"

He had never done that before, called his own daughter, or anyone else, a bitch. It must have been the weather. It made everybody irritable.

He joined her for a moment as she put Adam back in his crib. They watched their son thrash about and subside, munching contentedly on his pacifier. Carl slipped an arm around her waist.

She snuggled against him. "It won't be long now."

"What won't be long?" he asked.

"Till I see the doctor. You know, my six-week checkup."

"What's the significance of that?"

"Then we can—you know. We'll be back to normal." She spelled it out. "We can make love."

He smiled faintly, and drew away to tighten the sash on his bathrobe.

"It's been a long time," she reminded him.

A very long time. He seemed to be one of those men who had either a revulsion or a superstition about physical love with a pregnant woman. She had tried to assure him that it was all right, but still he hadn't liked the idea. And so she had waited. Soon, she thought, they would go back to the way it had been in the beginning. The way it should always be.

"She can't treat you like that," he said.

"Who, Mary Ellen?" She wished they were finished with Mary Ellen. "It's a bad age. What can you do? And a kind of mixed-up life for her."

"She's got a mixed-up mother."

"Yes, but in some ways you have to admire Barbara. She's very competent."

"Huh!" he snorted.

"Well, she's pretty good at making a career for herself.

But even with a career, she should give a little more of her time to Mary Ellen."

"It got to be more than I could take," he said. "All her neuroses."

"Do you think she's really bad for Mary Ellen? Why don't you try and get custody?"

For just a moment, she thought she saw a look of longing. Then he shook his head.

"Can't disrupt the kid any more. It's home for her, there in White Plains. All her friends, her school . . ."

He wanted Mary Ellen. Joyce had spoken rashly. But if it meant so much to Carl . . . And if Barbara was neurotic, and harmful . . . Before they were married, he had often talked to her about how he missed his daughter, how he saw her only during the day on certain weekends, because Barbara, being so neurotic, would never let her stay overnight. It was a tragic situation, Joyce had felt.

But later that evening she began to wonder if he really would be any improvement over Barbara. Mary Ellen arrived at the dinner table in a brief pair of shorts and a braless tee shirt that revealed her young breasts.

Carl's face turned pale. "What kind of outfit do you call that?"

"That's my clothes," Mary Ellen replied. "What do you want me to wear on a day like this?"

"It *is* hot," Joyce put in. Gail was wearing a similar outfit, but Gail did not have breasts or hips, and her legs were straight and little-girlish.

"I expect you to cover yourself," Carl said coldly.

Mary Ellen looked amazed. "Put on a *dress?*"

It occurred to Joyce that he must have been thinking of the murder. He did not want his daughter to be provocative. She beckoned to Mary Ellen, who followed her meekly up the stairs.

"What's the matter with him?" Mary Ellen demanded when they were safely in her room.

"Fathers are like that," Joyce explained. "Fathers of daughters. It's kind of old-fashioned, but they have their reasons. Have you got a slightly thicker shirt and maybe some longer pants?"

"But it's hot!"

"I know, dear, but— Has your mother bought you any bras?"

Mary Ellen groaned. "Oh, they're kidding, now they want to put me in a bra."

"Well, you ought to start thinking about it. But at least for now . . ." From the mess on the bed, Joyce picked up a dark blue shirt decorated with a picture of a van and a spattering of CB phrases. In all that clutter, no one would notice Mary Ellen's figure.

She persuaded the girl to put it on and they went back to the table. Carl glanced at his daughter and said nothing. Evidently he approved.

Hours later, as she lay in bed, Joyce thought again of what he had said. *It was more than I could take—all her neuroses.*

When they first began dating, she had asked about his divorce. From what little he said, she gathered that it was Barbara who had initiated the breakup, and that he had not resisted. Today Barbara had more or less given the same impression.

Now he claimed that it was he who had ended it, and against her will. Was it self-protection this time, or had he, earlier, been trying to protect Barbara?

She felt him, warm and breathing beside her. It is my business, she told herself.

On the other hand, his relationship with Barbara was entirely separate from his relationship with Joyce. She and Barbara were two separate people, one wrong for him, and one apparently right. So maybe it was not her business.

She fell asleep and into fleeting dreams of the body Sheila had described. She saw it, red, skinned, and mangled, and dreamed of how it had gotten that way. Over and over again she relived the victim's last agony, and felt she would never be free of it.

7

The next day Carl was up and dressed, but not in his usual lawn-mowing clothes, while she lay in bed nursing Adam.

"Going to buy a paper," he explained.

"So early?"

It was a mile and a half into the village. They rarely bothered with a newspaper on Saturday, certainly not at seven A.M.

"Be back in a while." He closed the door softly. Minutes later she heard his car hum to life, then fade away. The garage was on the other side of the house. She hadn't heard its door slide open, or closed. She wondered if it stood open, like a gaping mouth, with all of them vulnerable in bed. Would she ever get used to this fear? It was worse than in the city, where their basement apartment had had window bars and only one entrance, and that was always locked.

She smiled, remembering how Carl had hated that apartment of hers, and worried, and begged her to move out. He had even suggested that she move in with him, but his was only a studio apartment, and besides, there was straitlaced Gail, who would never have approved unless they were married first.

She hadn't long to wonder about the garage door. He was back soon, as he had promised. He came straight upstairs with both the *Times* and the *Daily News* under his arm.

"Here," he said, opening the second section of the *Times*. "How do you like this? The only thing missing is your name."

"*My* name?"

"For reporting it."

Find Body of Missing Westchester Woman. It was date-lined Cedarville, N.Y. She skimmed the three-inch story. The woman was Joan Danner, eighteen years old. Missing since May 29. She remembered the name. Found by two children playing in the woods. Bound, gagged, shreds of clothing, apparently cut off. Body heavily mutilated.

"Thanks," she said, handing back the paper. "You've really made my day."

"I thought you'd be interested. You're the one who got this whole thing started."

"I'm not interested. I hate it. Can you imagine what that girl's family is going through?"

She put Adam back in his crib, then washed her face and slipped a peignoir over her sheer nightgown.

Carl had preceded her to the kitchen. It was almost as though he were avoiding the sight of her in that night-gown, until she had the peignoir in place. And yet it was a set he had given her when they were married. He had found it provocative then, the see-through film of pale peach. It must be her figure, she decided, still a little loose. She would have to start doing exercises.

He had already started the coffee maker and was frying bacon. It was a peaceful breakfast, with only the two of them. Even Gail had reached the age of sleeping late. Or perhaps she only did it to avoid Carl.

He finished his second cup of coffee and pushed back his chair. "Better get that lawn mowed."

"It's awfully early, Mr. Suburbanite." Even after a year, they were still getting used to the routine of lawns, clogged gutters, and oil burners.

"If I wait, the kids will be trampling it down and then it won't cut properly." He went upstairs to put on his lawn-mowing uniform, as she called it: grass-stained work pants and a pair of tattered sneakers.

As she loaded the dishwasher and set the table for the next sitting, Gail came downstairs in her thin, too-small pajamas and silently helped herself to half a bowl of cereal.

"There's bacon," said Joyce.

"Mmm," Gail muttered.

"Aren't we bright and sunny this morning."

"Mommy, did they find out who that person is?"

"What person? Oh—yes. It was one of those missing girls. The older one."

"I'm glad it wasn't Valerie."

"Who's Valerie?"

"That's the other girl that's missing. Anita's sister knows her. They're in the same class."

Outside, the lawn mower started with a roar. It drowned out her half-formed answer, which was just as well. *Good luck, Valerie.* She went upstairs to change her clothes.

The newspapers were still on the bed where Carl had left them. The Times was folded open to the article she had already seen. She turned the pages of the *News.*

MISSING GIRL FOUND DEAD. And a blurry photograph of Joan Danner in life, a smiling, oval-faced blonde.

An autopsy revealed that the hyoid bone in the throat was broken, which indicated death by strangulation. It seemed clear that the mutilation had been done afterward. In a sexual rage, perhaps. It could not be determined whether the girl had been raped.

Of course not. The body had been around since May 29.

A freak. A real freak. How did nature ever come up with things like that?

Quickly she put on her clothes, made the bed, and took the newspapers down to the living room. She did not want them in the same room with Adam. She placed them neatly on the coffee table—as Barbara said, Carl liked things neat—and glanced out at the lawn, where the mower stood alone in the middle of the half-cut grass.

8

He saw them moving about in the meadow, the shapes of men, and he knew what they were doing. They must have been all over the place, all through the woods, down by that little brook. Probably searching the ruins near Lattimer, the cellar that remained, filled with rubble and fallen beams from some long-ago fire; the old springhouse, and the newer garage. He switched off the mower and left it there—he could finish it later, this wouldn't take long—and walked toward the meadow.

By the time he reached the stone wall, they had vanished. He followed the path until he saw one, a cop. The man wore his summer uniform, a short-sleeved blue shirt, and mirrored sunglasses so you couldn't see his eyes. He had arms like a pair of clubs.

"Morning," said Carl.

"H'lo," said the policeman. "You live around here?"

"Right over there." Carl nodded toward his house. "Gilwood's the name. You picked a nice hot day to be out here trekking through the woods."

"Didn't exactly pick it," the policeman replied. "It picked me."

Clichés were a sign of a limited mind. Carl managed to conceal his distaste.

"What are you looking for?" he asked. "The other little girl?"

The mirrored glasses reflected the sky. "What other little girl?"

"The other one that's missing. Isn't there another girl missing?"

"Got no way of knowing she's anywhere around here," said the cop. "Or even dead."

"Right. That's why you have to look, isn't it? Need any help?"

To his surprise, the cop accepted. "All the help we can get. You probably know this area better than we do."

"Be glad to. I was in the middle of cutting my grass." He hated to think of that scraggly, unfinished lawn. But this could be important.

"When you guys get thirsty," he suggested, "how about coming over to my place for a beer?"

"Thanks," said the cop, "but we got rules about that."

Carl didn't have his full attention. The man kept looking off in the distance, studying the trees, the knolls, the rocks—at least as far as you could tell from behind those glasses.

He wasn't going to find it there. Not in the trees.

"Coke, then," Carl said, as a way of calling him back. "We've got kids, we have plenty of soft drinks. My wife'll even make you some iced tea. It's her specialty, that powdered stuff."

The cop granted him a moment of notice. "That's real nice. Maybe we'll take you up on it." Somebody must have flattened his nose once. It had a pushed-in look.

"Meantime," Carl reminded him, "you'd better tell me what we're looking for."

"Anything. But just look. Don't touch. Don't disturb anything. Mostly what we're trying to find right now is some sort of cool place. A cave or a cellar, something like that."

"What do you want a cave or a cellar for?"

"Want to know where the body was kept. The girl disappeared the end of May. You got a strong stomach? The corpse wasn't as far gone as you'd expect in that time."

"Really," said Carl. "What makes you think she died the day she disappeared?"

"We're not ruling out anything. It's just not so easy to keep somebody a prisoner without people knowing."

"Okay. And how's it going to help if you find this place?"

"It'll help. Now remember, don't touch anything. That's important. I appreciate this, Mr. Gilwood."

What a farce, Carl thought as he and three other men

fanned out across the meadow, looking for rocks and cave formations—when he knew there weren't any.

Small-town cops. Probably never had any case bigger than a lost dog before.

Down over the next stone wall he could hear the gurgle of the brook. He wondered how long it would take them to start thinking about that brook.

9

As assiduously as he scoured the woods and fields, Frank D'Amico watched the people who were temporarily and informally under his command. Some were only high school kids out for a little adventure. Others were rednecks from the lower village, eager to "get" the killer. They were the kind who saw the victim less as a woman than a stolen object.

Both those types bore watching. So did the people who lived in the immediate area. There was Foster Farand, an unassuming-looking man with a big voice and slight build. D'Amico had known him for many years, but that didn't let him out of the picture.

There was that Gilwood guy, relatively new in the community. Even with the grass stains on his pants, Frank had him pegged as a compulsive man, a very controlled sort of person. Too controlled, perhaps.

It was Gilwood's wife who had reported finding the corpse, he remembered.

Then there was the big fellow Cheskill, a brute of a body if ever he saw one, but mild enough on the surface. Except you never could tell what lay below the surface.

"Hey, Chief, I think we've got something here."

That was Finneran. Without betraying anything, Frank sent his searchers down the brook, away from its source, and followed Arthur up the slope to the Lattimer ruins.

It was cold inside that shed where the spring bubbled up, like being in a refrigerator on a hot summer day. A scrap of white fabric lay in the dirt, and in one corner, with his flashlight, Herb Mackey had caught the glitter of something that might have been part of an earring.

They couldn't tell about the floor, not without a lab test. There was something on it—or in it, rather, since it was a dirt floor, but it could have been anything. They might have used the room for slaughtering chickens a hundred years ago, it looked that old.

"Okay, you guys," he said to Finneran and Mackey, "we've got a big one here, and we're keeping it to ourselves. We're going to watch this place day and night, and nobody's going to know about it. That includes the newspapers, the mayor, and especially those civilians out there, understand?"

They understood. They were good men, even if they'd never worked on anything like this before.

"Think maybe the guy is going to try and come back?" Mackey asked.

"You never know. Every one of those guys is aware we're looking for a place like this. If he's one of them, he might want to come back and check it over."

"You don't think it's Lattimer," said Finneran.

"I'm not playing it by guesswork."

"That guy gives me the creeps." Finneran crawled to the door of the hut and looked out. "He's standing up there watching us and he hasn't said a word all day."

"Can he see us now?" asked Frank.

"I don't think so. But here we are, going all over his property—he owns this place, doesn't he?"

"He knows what we're doing. We have what they call his 'tacit consent.' And it's tacit, all right."

"You didn't get a search warrant, did you?" Finneran needled. D'Amico did not reply. He poked around further, although there was nothing else in the hut, or shed, or whatever it was, except bits of debris from ages past, and the captive spring where the brook came to life and started its run down the slope into the woods.

He'd have to get some lab boys in here. He hadn't any of his own, he'd have to borrow some, but the first thing to do was clear those civilians out of the area so as not to arouse their suspicion about the place. So far, it was the only lead they had.

He didn't worry about Lattimer. The old man wouldn't talk to anyone. He never spoke at all except to chase people away, maybe once or twice a year. Even when he walked into town for his groceries, he was quiet as a clam. Whether he was the killer or not—and Frank doubted it, although they couldn't rule him out—at least he wouldn't go around blabbing that the police had been in one of his outbuildings. Or all of them, actually.

Herb Mackey said, "Chief, I just thought of something."

"What's that?" Frank studied the earring without picking it up.

"That piece of white cloth there. In the missing person report, Joan Danner wasn't wearing anything white. And the kid, Valerie Cruz, had a white blouse."

Frank rocked back on his heels. He knew Valerie Cruz. He had watched her cross that big intersection on her way to school every morning. Every day, where three main streets crossed. she had made it safely, from the year she was in kindergarten and let go of her mother's hand for the first time. Every day—for what?

It didn't mean anything, of course, just because a piece of white cloth turned up in some frigid, musty shed. But it figured. They had found the one girl and there were two of them missing.

"Damn," said Herb Mackey. "The kid's father and her brother are out there with those civilians."

10

Carl was up just as early again the next morning. It made a little more sense for the Sunday paper, but seven o'clock seemed a bit unnecessary. Joyce was surprised they even had it printed by then, much less that the drugstore was open at that hour.

She roused herself when she heard his car drive away. This time she had reminded him to close the garage door. The request seemed to amaze him. But he had been willing to do anything she asked, for today his mother was being inflicted upon her.

"And I don't mind telling you," she said to Adam, who stared at her with misty blue eyes, "your grandmother scares me to death."

Cold and critical was Olivia Terry Gilwood Dunn. And yet she must have had a human streak, inviting herself over to see all two of her grandchildren for the first time under one roof. Or had Carl invited her?

No, not all her grandchildren. Joyce tended to forget about Daniella, Carl's older sister, who lived in Tucson and had three nearly grown children of her own. It was easy to forget Daniella, for Carl never had anything to do with her, although each year she sent him a beautiful, homemade Christmas card. When he spoke of her, he spoke ruefully. Joyce often wondered what Daniella had done to earn that rue, but he would never tell her.

She was in the kitchen setting up the coffee maker when he returned.

"It's funny," he said, "they didn't find anything yesterday, even with all those people looking around. If you ask me, it was a big fake. The police sent them on a wild-goose chase."

"What did you expect them to find?" she asked.

48

"I know what they were looking for. The other little girl. But the police weren't going to admit it. They tried to throw everybody off the track."

She did not reply. It bothered her when he talked that way. He sounded almost paranoid. The best thing to do was ignore him.

After breakfast, she went upstairs to dress. Gail emerged sleepily from her room. "Mommy, is Olivia coming today?"

"Yes, honey. I think she's probably 'Mrs. Dunn' to you."

"I don't care. I'm not going to call her anything. I'm not going to talk to her."

Carl bellowed from the foot of the stairs, "Are those kids up yet?"

"One of them is," Joyce replied.

"What about Mary Ellen? Dammit, her grandmother's coming." He climbed the stairs two at a time and flung open Mary Ellen's door. Joyce caught a glimpse of a thin pink nightgown and a sheet pulled hastily over it.

"What do you think you're doing," he thundered, "wasting everybody's time lolling in bed? Get up and get dressed."

She answered with a little squeal, "I'm not wasting anybody's time except my own."

"You get up and get your clothes on. Your grandmother's coming."

Gail, rummaging through a dresser drawer, asked, "Mommy, where are my blue shorts?"

"Probably in the laundry," Joyce replied.

"Why didn't you wash them?"

"I haven't had time. There's been too much going on around here."

"I don't have anything to *wear*."

Carl, his attention drawn from Mary Ellen, stood observing the exchange. "Just why are you giving your mother a hard time " he inquired.

"Because she didn't do the laundry, and I don't have any clothes."

Joyce said, "You must have something."

"Well, I don't!" Stamping into the bathroom, Gail

raged, "I'll take my dirty stuff out of the hamper. It's all your fault!"

Carl made a dive for her, seized her by the arm and gave her bottom a loud slap.

"That's for being fresh with your mother," he said, as drops of perspiration appeared on his forehead.

Gail stared at him in speechless outrage. Then she fled to her room, gasping in huge sobs, and slammed the door.

Joyce said, "You didn't have to spank her, Carl."

"I don't like her talking to you that way."

"But to spank her?"

"How else is she going to learn?" He seemed quite calm, now that he had blown off steam. But Gail needed a chance to blow off, too.

"I know she was fresh," Joyce sighed, "but I hardly think it was worth a spanking. And I do understand how she feels, with Adam, and your mother, and Mary Ellen. It's all your family. She feels left out. That's really what she was saying."

"Listen," he said, "forget about 'my' family. We're all one family now. I acted in loco parentis."

"What's that?" she asked grudgingly.

" 'In place of a parent.' And I'll thank you to back me up. Otherwise we'll have a bunch of outlaws on our hands." He turned abruptly and went downstairs.

Gail's door remained closed. Joyce knocked softly, and from inside, heard a sob. She opened it a crack. "Honey?"

Gail lay on the bed, her face puffed with tears. Joyce sat down and tried to take the unyielding body into her arms.

"Honey, I'm sorry Carl's in such a rotten mood. He just yelled at Mary Ellen, too. I think he's nervous because of Olivia coming."

"He—spanked—me," Gail sobbed.

"Yes, but I'm sure he didn't mean to."

"I *hate* him."

Gail felt very thin and small inside her pajamas, and had taken such a buffeting from life. My fault, thought her mother. She hoped Carl would come to his senses and apologize. But she knew Carl. He might come to his senses, but never apologize.

She had given Adam his mid-morning feeding, which

was gradually working its way closer to noon, when Olivia arrived in her banana-colored Granada.

Carl, Joyce, and Mary Ellen trooped outside to meet her. Olivia looked crisp in a white dress with green polka dots, a string of pearls, and packages under her arm.

"There's dear Mary Ellen," she caroled as they enveloped her and led her around by the flagstone path to the front door. "How are you, dear? How's your summer?" She planted a dry kiss on Mary Ellen's cheek.

"Oh, fine." Mary Ellen danced along beside her. "It's okay here, and Adam's adorable, and yesterday there were police all over looking for a body and Daddy went out to help. Gail and I went, too, but they wouldn't let us help."

Frowning slightly, Carl said, "I told you about that on the phone." Joyce hadn't known he had phoned his mother last night, probably to prepare her for this.

"It was in the newspapers, too," said Mary Ellen.

Olivia asked, "Are you sure you want to go on living here?"

"Why not?" said Carl. "It's home. That kind of thing can happen anywhere."

"Well . . ." Olivia presented her cheek to Carl. His kiss was as dry as hers had been. She handed the smaller of her two packages to Mary Ellen. "For you. And this one's for Adam. Where is Adam?"

"I just put him to bed," said Joyce.

In a hushed herd, they went up the stairs. Adam, still awake after his feeding, blinked at them and kicked his legs. Olivia reached into the crib. "Hello, darling. Come to Grandma." She scooped him up and held him stiffly.

Mary Ellen stroked the baby's arm. "He's so precious. I can hardly believe he's my brother."

"He doesn't even look like you," Olivia said. "You take after your mother." She bounced him up and down and he spewed his lunch onto her shoulder.

"What have you been feeding this child?" Hastily she handed him to Joyce and suffered Carl to clean off her dress.

"Oh, what a shame," said Joyce. "He did just have a full meal. I guess that sudden motion wasn't good for him."

Carl escorted Olivia downstairs for a glass of sherry while Joyce returned the baby to his crib.

When she went to join them, Carl had poured drinks for the two women and was in the kitchen mixing one for himself. She could hear him opening a tray of ice cubes, spilling them like rocks into the plastic bin in the freezing compartment. Olivia sat across from her, gazing at the mantelpiece.

The silence was nerve-wracking. Casting about for something to say, Joyce surprised herself by asking. "Have you heard from Daniella recently?"

Olivia, her attention jerked from the mantel, stared at her suspiciously They had never discussed Daniella before. Or much of anything. They had never, Joyce realized, even been alone together before.

"I frequently hear from Daniella," Olivia replied. "Why?"

"I just wondered. We got a card from her at Christmas, but I don't think Carl sent her one. He hardly ever talks about her. Sometimes I forget he even has a sister."

"She's out in Arizona. That's a fairly good distance."

"Yes, but—"

"How often do you talk about your sister? I suppose you have a sister or brother."

"Two sisters and two brothers," said Joyce, expecting then to be asked about her family.

But Olivia did not care about her family. She rested her sherry glass on the arm of her chair and again studied the mantel.

"Carl and Daniella used to be very close, when they were growing up. But it's hardly appropriate to stay that attached to one another, do you think?"

"It depends," Joyce said. "It's a different kind of closeness. I feel, with my brother Pat—well, he's a good friend." She excused herself, called the girls to set the table, and went out to the kitchen, where Carl was measuring vermouth into his glass.

"What on earth are you doing?" she asked.

"Mixing a drink. What's the matter, can't you talk to her?"

"It's not easy." She opened the refrigerator and took out a bowl of chicken that was marinating in lime juice. "Everything I say, she argues with. Everything she says, it sounds as if she's trying to pick a fight with me."

"Aren't you exaggerating a little?"

She motioned him to keep his voice low, and began arranging the chicken on a broiling pan.

"Well, that's the way it seems. It just seems hostile, the way she talks to me."

He rattled his drink and tasted it. "I suppose it's possible that you resent her, because she had me before you did."

"I certainly do not! After all, she's your mother. I'm not in competition with her."

Or was she?

Trying to ease over the argument, she said, "I don't know, maybe I'm just moody. It must be the heat."

"It's postpartum depression."

"Baloney. I don't get that."

"Very experienced, aren't you? Anyway, it's more apt to happen with the second than the first, didn't you know? Probably you miss something about your old life. That's what it often is."

"I don't miss anything." She wondered if that was true.

"You're sure?"

She remembered the summer mornings on the fringes of Greenwich Village, even in that cramped apartment . . . the lazy walks to buy a newspaper—yes, Larry had been around sometimes . . . the antique shops that were open on Sunday, where they could browse and dream . . . and sunning on the pier in the Hudson River. She tried to remember the soot, and the times Larry wasn't there.

"Of course not. I told you."

Gail drifted down the stairs, pale-faced and miserable. All through the meal she remained a silent tragic figure, so that this time it was fortunate that no one took the trouble to notice her.

She was released after dinner when they moved into the sun porch with their coffee. Mary Ellen stayed with them, alternately listening to the grown-up talk and staring out of the window, her eyes glazed with boredom.

Olivia stirred sugar into her coffee. "I hear you got a Christmas card from Daniella and you didn't send her one. What's the matter with you?"

"Just didn't think of it," Carl answered with a smile.

Joyce said, "I would have sent her one, but I didn't know her address."

"Is that why you don't write?" Olivia asked. "You lost her address?"

"I have it someplace," he replied.

"And you used to be so close."

Joyce said, "I think we ought to keep in touch. We might like to visit her sometime. I've never seen the Southwest."

Carl asked in astonishment, "What on earth do you want to visit Daniella for?"

"They used to be so close," Olivia repeated, "after their father and I were divorced. It's a shame."

A reversal of her earlier thesis.

"How old were they?" Joyce asked. She really knew very little about Carl's early life.

"Let's see. Carl was four, I think, when we separated, and Daniella was nine. No, wait, it was later. I married again two years later, you know."

"I knew you'd married again." Only because Olivia had a different last name. "But what do you mean 'it was later'?"

"The time I'm talking about. It was after I remarried. I was with Carl a lot in those two years in between—he was so little—then I married again. Daniella was eleven. She took over for me then. She was almost a mother to him. But I suppose he grew up after a while and didn't need a mother."

Joyce glanced at Carl and found him watching Mary Ellen.

His coffee cup began to rattle in its saucer and he set it down. "Haven't you anything decent to wear?" he demanded of his daughter.

Mary Ellen's jaw dropped. "This *is* decent. What do you want me to do, wear a blanket? Honestly, Daddy."

"Carl, really, it is hot," Joyce reminded him, and her words sounded familiar. They had been through all that the other day.

Tight-lipped, he replied, "It's the way she was bending over."

"Well, I'm sorry I don't have a bra," Mary Ellen sulked. "I'm sorry I can't stay six years old forever."

Joyce reached out to pat her arm. "You don't want to be six years old forever." How fortunate that Mary Ellen accepted her own maturing process, even if her father did not.

Furiously he hissed, "Joyce, mind your own business."

She was silent, chastened. This was between father and daughter—but so irrational. It would only hurt Mary Ellen, and Carl, too, in the long run.

I'll get her some bras, she decided. If Barbara can't be bothered, I can.

She thought again of the murder and how helpless it must make him feel with a growing daughter, a phenomenon men never seemed to understand or take for granted.

Olivia watched them all with a forced little smile.

11

Mary Ellen was enchanted by her young brother, if not by anything else in the household. She leaned over the bathinette watching him kick, and held the spray hose while Joyce soaped his body.

"He's so tiny," she exclaimed. "Was he even smaller when he was born?"

"He was scrawnier," said Joyce. "They usually are. But actually he was rather big for a newborn. Eight pounds, three ounces." She lifted Adam from the bathinette and wrapped him in a towel. Downstairs, the telephone rang.

"Can I hold him while you answer it?" Mary Ellen asked.

Joyce picked up the phone in the bedroom. Immediately Barbara's agitated voice sputtered over the wire.

"Listen, I just heard on the radio they found a *second* body right where you are. A *second* body. I didn't hear anything about a first one."

"Another? I didn't—When was this?"

"Yesterday. You mean you didn't know?"

"About the first one, yes. But not— Where was it? Did they say?"

"Just 'in the same area.' Now, what first? Was it anywhere near you? Was it one of those missing girls?"

"Yes, the older one. It was in the newspaper, Barbara."

"I was away for the weekend. Now tell me, how near you?"

"Not right here. Maybe half a mile, I don't know." Joyce exaggerated the distance, for Barbara's sake. Why hadn't they told her about the second body? "They," she supposed, being the police.

"I know exactly how you feel," she said. "I have a

56

daughter, too, but believe me, these kids stay right around the house."

Mary Ellen, holding Adam bundled in her arms, sat watching from the rocking chair in a corner of the room. "Is that my mother?"

Joyce nodded, and looked out at the sunshine on the lawn, at the bright meadow with its daisies, and the apple tree. It couldn't be happening. Not here.

Maybe I should get a dog, she thought.

Barbara said, "Anyway, that's not the problem. Is my daughter there now?"

"Yes, do you want to talk to her?"

Not the problem? Joyce wondered as she finished dressing Adam. If that wasn't the problem, what was?

"No, I don't want to," Mary Ellen was saying into the phone. After a pause, during which snatches of Barbara's voice crackled across the room, she explained, "There's nothing to do. There's nothing to do here, either, but at least it's a little more fun. I helped Joyce give the baby his bath."

Moments later she hung up, wrinkling her face in disgust. "I don't know what's the matter with that woman."

"You can't really blame her," Joyce said. "She's concerned about you. She must miss you very much."

"That'll be the day. She's got something bothering her. It's always something."

Mary Ellen remained transfixed while Adam was fed his mashed banana. He was propped in a reclining seat on the kitchen table, with Mary Ellen gazing in adoration at his messy face, when footsteps thumped light on the walk outside.

Anita peered through the screen door. "Mrs. Gilwood, did you know they found Valerie Cruz and she's dead, too? She was in my sister's class."

"I heard," said Joyce. "It's horrible. And I'm amazed that your mother allows you to wander around alone, even on the road. Does she know you're here?"

"I guess so." Anita let herself in. "Valerie was a friend of my sister's, and when they found her, she was all cut up. They cut open her stomach and took out all her, you know, what's inside. I bet *that* hurt."

"I bet she was already dead when they did it," Joyce

said. Gail, coming into the kitchen at the sound of Anita's voice, turned ashen. Joyce added, "I'd rather we didn't talk about those things."

"They killed her by choking her to death," Anita went on. "Like this." She reached for Gail's throat. Gail slapped her away.

Anita was taken aback by Gail's hostile reaction, but soon recovered. She ran squealing up the stairs, with Gail after her, and brought down the dolls to play with on the lawn.

By that time, some of the lawn was in shade. Joyce carried a lunch tray outside to a small wooden table under an oak tree. She found the two girls huddled by the zinnia bed. Anita's voice drifted over to her ". . . go back to that place."

"No," said Gail.

"But I have to get my peacock and my horse. I left them there, remember? And you were there, too, so it's partly your fault, and you have to go with me."

Gail looked at her mother in mute appeal. To distract them from whatever Anita was trying to cook up, Joyce said, "After lunch, maybe we can go swimming. All of us."

Gail was delighted, almost to the point of forgetting about the murders. They packed away the dolls and ate their lunch, then set out in the car, with Adam's travel bed in the back seat. Mary Ellen squeezed herself in beside it. Gail and Anita sat in front.

They stopped at the Farands' house so that Anita could change into her swimsuit. Sheila came out to the car and leaned on the window.

"I suppose you heard the news?"

"If you mean about the other girl, yes. I heard it this morning."

"I just can't believe it. My daughter knew that kid. Joyce, what are we going to do?"

"What can we do? Just watch out, I guess."

"Oh, you, you're a city girl. You're used to these things."

"I'm both. I grew up in the country, and believe it or not, I never felt any worse off in the city. We always had

our door locked, and there were always people around. I
felt—"

Not safe, after Larry died. She had hated it then.

Anita came out of the house wearing a pair of shorts
over her suit, and got into the car. They drove through the
edge of Cedarville, past a row of small stores and modest
houses. After that, the street diminished to a narrow winding road that led out into the country. About a mile later,
they came to an artificial pond with the pretentious name
of Paradise Lake. The entrance fee was immodest, but it
was the only place near Cedarville where they could swim.
She settled herself with Adam in a grove of pine trees and
watched the girls play in the water. Anita had latched onto
Mary Ellen and was whispering to her and giggling, which
left Gail by herself.

But Gail often played and swam alone. She paddled
near the shore, humming softly, and found pebbles and
flip tops to create another microcosm, as she had created
the fairy house. Mary Ellen, who turned out to be a surprisingly good swimmer, abandoned Anita and double-
overarmed to a large float near the center of the pond,
occupied by a group of teenagers. Joyce watched in mild
alarm as Mary Ellen quickly befriended a romantically
dark youth with the body of a man. They swam around
the raft, dove off it, raced, and splashed each other.

Gail came out of the water and stood shivering by her
mother.

"You're freezing." Joyce handed her a towel.

"Mommy, I don't like it anymore."

"Why not?"

"I don't like the bottom of it. It's all muddy, and there
are sticks and things."

The bottom of it, which she could not see . . . She
could only feel the mud and the sticks. Gail was cursed
with too much imagination. Now even this was spoiled for
her.

Gail settled under the trees, wrapped in her towel. But
Anita, who was incapable of playing alone, came to in-
veigle her back into the water.

"I'll race you," she coaxed. Gail shook her head.

"Well, *I'm* going in the water, and *I'm* going to have

fun." Anita rolled about, wiggled her toes, and performed enticing antics. She had chosen a shallow area where sand from the artificial beach could still be seen through two feet of water. It was clear of mud and sticks. Gail wandered down to the shore. Ignoring Anita, she stepped into the water until it covered her feet.

Anita barrel-rolled on the sandy bottom. Gail waded into deeper water. Anita turned a somersault. Gail stared at the trees on the opposite shore.

Suddenly Anita was on Gail's back. They both tumbled into the water. Then only Anita emerged, riding on something and laughing wildly.

Joyce kicked off her shoes and splashed into the lake. A young woman in a blue bikini ran with her, blowing a whistle. She pulled Gail from the water and led her toward the beach, where a crowd of children gathered to stare.

Gail sputtered and choked. The woman patted her on the back until she seemed to be breathing evenly.

The children drifted away, except for Anita, who stood gaping at Gail. On catching Joyce's eye, she giggled self-consciously.

"That wasn't funny," Joyce said. "Why did you do it, Anita?"

"Because she wouldn't play with me."

Gail was still choking and trying to clear her throat. Anita watched her curiously.

Joyce asked, "Do you think that's the way to get someone to play with you?"

Anita tilted her head and pulled on a strand of hair, trying coquetry where it had no chance of succeeding.

"My father does that sometimes."

"He ducks you? Gail could have drowned!"

She should have ignored the statement. Anita was a known liar, trying to justify herself.

It wasn't possible, not the mild-mannered Foster Farand, with his rimless glasses, his bald spot, and funny little smile.

No, Anita herself was crazy and vicious. Or only childish and unthinking?

On the other hand, could there be something wrong

with Foster? Something she had never seen? But not even Foster—Not that.

And yet, there had been two murders. Where there were murders, there was a killer.

It had to be somebody.

12

Anita, sensing that she was out of favor, tried a different approach. She became sweetly contrite—and emptily so, it seemed to Joyce—stroking Gail's arm and trying to jolly her out of her silence, but never quite apologizing.

"You had the lifeguard come and save you," she purred. "Were you scared in the water?"

Gail regarded her stonily.

"My father does that to me all the time," Anita said. "You get used to it after a while."

Gail glanced at her mother. Joyce smiled and winked. The response was too frivolous. Gail turned away, feeling betrayed there, too.

Joyce saw Mary Ellen swimming back from the float, and decided it would be a good time to leave.

As they walked toward the parking lot, Anita announced to everyone's distress, "I'm supposed to go home with you until my mother calls. She's going out shopping, and she's scared for me to be in the house when nobody's there. I always used to stay home alone. I think she's crazy. It's because of those dead girls. It makes people crazy." She giggled.

"I don't really think it's awfully funny," Joyce reproached her. "Those were living girls, just like you, and now they won't ever have any more life. It's not fun or exciting."

Anita sobered on the surface, but her eyes twinkled. She skipped ahead, to show how unafraid she was.

Gail muttered, "I don't like her."

Mary Ellen stopped abruptly. "Uh-oh,".

"Did you forget something?" asked Joyce.

"No. I shouldn't have gone in the water. I think I've got it."

"Got it? Oh, my heavens." The problem was clear from the way Mary Ellen stood, with her thighs pressed tightly together.

"There's a little outhouse near the beach," Joyce said.

"But I don't have anything with me. I'll have to sit on a towel in the car." So saying, Mary Ellen wrapped her towel around her hips. "It always does this. It just comes on without any warning."

"How long have you been having it?"

"About half a year. I'm almost thirteen." In another half year. "I have this friend of mine who started when she was ten."

Their car shimmered in the sunlight and its door handles burned their fingers. The plastic seatcovers burned, too. They all had to sit on towels.

"Do you want to stop at a drugstore?" Joyce asked.

"No, I have some at home." Mary Ellen smiled, feeling a bond. They were both women together, while Gail stared at them, not quite understanding, and Anita sang, trying to attract attention.

Joyce drove past the Farands' house, hoping to get rid of Anita, but the house was locked and the car gone. She wondered if she ought to tell Sheila what had happened at the lake. But what good would it do? Would Sheila want to know her child was vicious, and could she help it?

And if it was true about Foster, Sheila probably already knew that. What a mess it all was.

When they reached home, Mary Ellen showered and dressed and settled in her room to catch up on her school reading list, as she explained. Gail went to her own room, but it was invaded by Anita, who did not wish to be ignored. The child was almost schizophrenic, the way she seemed to have no idea of the undesirability of what she had done.

Joyce left it up to Gail to handle it. Gail's distaste was bound to have more effect than anything anyone else could do or say, and besides, Adam was hungry.

And she was tired. The heat had done her in. From the peace of her own room, as Adam nursed, she heard Mary Ellen's radio playing its endless disco beat. She fell asleep before Adam did and slept away two hours with the baby in the crook of her arm.

They woke together. She thought the house seemed very quiet, and wondered whether it was morning or afternoon, and where everybody was.

A look at the clock gave her her bearings. They had gone swimming, she now remembered, and Anita had tried to drown Gail. She did not want to recall that part of it. There had once been a time when she was fond of Anita's parents, but now everything was mixed up, you couldn't trust anybody.

Anita had apparently left, thank God. Gail was alone in her room, playing with tiny plasticene dolls that she had made herself.

"Gail, where's Mary Ellen?"

"I don't know."

"She doesn't seem to be in the house. Did she go out?"

"I don't know." A little more impatiently this time.

"Well, now look. If she went out, where would she go?"

"Mommy, I *don't know*."

There was nothing within walking distance except other houses, and Mary Ellen did not know any of the people in them.

"Did she go with Anita?"

"No," said Gail, "Anita went home with her mother."

Might she have gone to the woods to see where the bodies had been? She hadn't seemed all that interested, but one never knew. And what if she ran into the killer?

No, she wouldn't, Joyce thought. She wouldn't.

Carl would be home soon. And if the girl wasn't found by then . . .

She called the Farands' house. Denise answered the phone. It seemed only logical that Mary Ellen might have gone to visit Denise. They were the same age, although they barely knew each other. But Denise had not seen her.

They can't do this to me. Joyce felt an irrational anger at Gail. If the two girls had been in better communication, Mary Ellen would surely have told her where she was going. Gail only made her feel unwelcome.

She walked around the outside of the house, trying to see into the meadow, into the woods in back of the house. She dared not leave the children, dared not herself venture into the wilderness.

The meadow was a blaze of late afternoon light and

filled with buzzing insects. A butterfly danced over the daisies.

She called from the stone wall. "Mary Ellen?"

Damn, the girl was just at the wrong age. And menstruating, too. What if he found that out? Would he let her go? Or would it enrage him?

She went back to the house. Carl was already late, it was seven o'clock. She prayed his train would be delayed, sitting on the tracks somewhere. She prayed for Mary Ellen's safety.

Gail leaned over the stair rail and asked plaintively where she had been.

"Out looking for Mary Ellen," Joyce replied. "Are you sure she didn't say anything about where she was going?"

Gail looked hurt. "I'm telling the truth."

"I know you are, honey. I just thought there might have been something you forgot."

"Well, I didn't, and I don't know why you're making so much fuss about Mary Ellen. She's twelve years old."

Gail paused, apparently reminded that so was Valerie Cruz. Joyce could read it on her face.

"Mommy, is anything going to happen?"

"If she doesn't get home before her father does, something will certainly happen." Take Gail's mind off the murders. "And I just hope he doesn't blame me too much, but I *am* responsible for her."

"I'll protect you," Gail crooned in a dreamy voice. She would have loved a chance to take on Carl and defeat him. Then she asked, "What are we having for dinner?"

Joyce was appalled at the irrelevance of it, but realized she hadn't even thought about dinner, and Carl would be coming any minute. It was too late to thaw anything, but she found a can of salmon in the cupboard. Salmon loaf was a good last-minute standby, although it had to cook for an hour.

After the loaf was in the oven, she turned on the radio to find out whether there were any train delays. Not that she worried about Carl—she only hoped he would be delayed until Mary Ellen came back. Damn that girl, anyway.

What if something did happen? And here I am, cursing her.

The heat had gotten to her, and so had the murders. She took another tour around the house while Gail set the table. The salmon loaf finished cooking and still neither Carl nor Mary Ellen appeared. They ate a bleak, nearly silent dinner, while the sun went down.

Now the meadow was gray in the twilight. She couldn't be out this late, after dark.

And Carl, too. Where was he? The radio had said nothing about a serious delay on the railroad. If he had to work late, he should have called.

She jumped at the sound of voices outside the kitchen door. Mary Ellen came in, alone.

"Good God, Mary Ellen, where were you? It's been hours, and it's dark outside."

"Is Daddy here?" Mary Ellen seemed to be listening.

"Not yet, and you can be very grateful for that. Now, where were you?" Joyce went to the door and in the gathering darkness saw a slim youthful figure walking quickly down the driveway.

"Who's that?"

"A boy. His name's David. He was at the lake this afternoon."

"Does he live near here?"

"No, he has a motorcycle. He left it out on the road because I thought Daddy was home. He took me riding and it was gorgeous. We were out all afternoon."

"I hope you realize—"

"Joyce, don't spoil it. It was so gorgeous, with the wind on my face. It was like flying without an airplane."

"Mary Ellen, I don't want you to disappear like that without telling me where you're going."

Mary Ellen tossed her hair in a gesture reminiscent of Anita. "I can't see what difference it makes where I'm going."

"It makes a huge difference that I know where you are. I wanted to go out and look for you and I didn't even know where to begin."

Amusement flitted across the girl's face. "I'm glad you didn't. I'd have died." She started into the living room.

"Yes," said Joyce, catching her arm, "you might have. Don't you understand? Two young women have been killed right here in this area. Don't you *understand?*"

"I was okay." Mary Ellen twitched irritably and tried to squirm free.

"And that boy you were with. We don't even know him. He could have been—"

Another toss of the hair. "I know him."

"Mary Ellen—" Joyce let go of the arm, even knowing her captive might vanish. "What do you think your father's going to say about all this?"

"You wouldn't tell him!" She had finally gotten through to the child. "He's so strict."

"Maybe he should be."

"Please, Joyce? It was so beautiful. You'll ruin my beautiful day."

Joyce wavered. She had the upper hand now, and she used it to extract a promise that this would never happen again.

Mary Ellen ate a tablespoonful of salmon loaf, then went to her room to dream of David and motorcycles. Joyce was clearing the table, leaving a place for Carl, when she heard his car in the driveway.

He was disheveled when he came in, and drenched with sweat, but he did not seem tired. His walk was energetic and his smile wide. He did not kiss her. It was too hot.

"What happened?" she asked, "Did you walk all the way from the city?"

"Walk?" he said vacantly, without seeming to hear her. "Some people came from out of town." Yes, he had been drinking, she could smell it. "I had to catch a late train, and the air conditioning broke down."

"Oh, poor baby. Do you want me to wash your suit?" She reached for his jacket, which he carried balled under his arm.

He clamped onto it, refusing to give it up. "That's okay. Just leave it."

"But you can't wear it again like this. You're soaked."

"It's okay. I'll take care of it. You've had enough to do all day." He started up the stairs.

"Do you want any dinner?" she asked.

"Maybe, in a while."

She heard the shower running for a long time and then he went down to the laundry room to put his clothes in the washer. When he came back up, his forehead and up-

per lip were already covered with new droplets of sweat.
Even though the sun had gone down, a soggy blanket of
warm humidity remained.

"I really could have done that for you," she said. "It's
no trouble at all. I could have started it while you took
your shower."

"You never use the wash-and-wear cycle," he explained.
"I like my suit done just right."

"But if you put it in the dryer anyway, you don't need
the wash-and-wear cycle. It all comes out the same."

"What have we here?" He sat down at the table.
"Salmon loaf. You haven't made that in a long time."

"It might be a little dry. I had to reheat it."

"Doesn't matter a bit, with that good sauce." He was in
a very genial mood, considering his ordeal on the train.

Mary Ellen walked through the dining room, wearing a
pair of cut-off jeans and a tee shirt. She glanced at her father and crossed her arms over her breasts. He paid no attention. A moment later Joyce could hear her talking on
the kitchen telephone, probably to David. She almost com-
mented lightly that Mary Ellen had a boyfriend, but she
bit back the words. Some fathers might be amused, but
not Carl. And especially not when Mary Ellen was only
twelve.

Besides, how could they tell about David? Or anybody?
David looked too young and innocent to do the things the
killer had done, but you couldn't be sure. A man's sexual
drive and powers were supposed to be at their peak in the
late teens.

The call was short. Mary Ellen had started to leave the
kitchen when the phone rang behind her. She picked it up.

"For you, Daddy. It's Grandmother."

"Thanks, kid." He went into the kitchen and sat on one
of the dinette chairs, rocking it onto its back legs. His
buoyant mood seemed to extend even to Olivia. He
greeted her with an easy "Hiya. How are you?" listened
for a moment, and then said cheerfully, "Nope. Can't
make it."

Thank heaven, thought Joyce. For once he was not at
his mother's beck and call. Then he said, "Well, you know,
I'll be taking my vacation in a couple of weeks. Maybe we
could see you then."

She was shocked. When he hung up, she asked, "Why didn't you tell me about your vacation?"

He was still thinking of the phone call. "Some friends of hers are going to be there this weekend and she wanted us to come over. I'll be damned if I feel like seeing her friends."

"But why didn't you tell *me* about your vacation? How come your mother gets to know before I do?"

"There you go, jealous again." He carefully straightened the chair he had sat on. "It just came through. I knew we couldn't go anywhere because of the baby, so I didn't put myself on the schedule, but it just happens that's a good time."

"Why can't we go anywhere?"

"With a baby?"

She was still resentful and acting childish. Of course he was right. The baby was too young to be dragged around, and it would be a nuisance with all the special equipment they would have to take.

"Nothing wrong with home," he said.

"No, I guess not." Cedarville was a beautiful place. If she wanted to see more of the world, it could wait until the children were older.

She started the dishwasher and then went upstairs to take her bath. He had come home so late it was almost bedtime, and there was still Adam to feed, and Adam sometimes woke her at two A.M.

Before she could fall asleep, Carl came in and sat on the edge of the bed. Her flesh waited for his touch. She was surprised at the anticipation she felt. Like a girl making love for the first time.

He did not reach out. He simply asked, "Then is it okay with you if we go and see Olivia while I'm on vacation, as long as her friends aren't around?"

"What's wrong with her friends?"

Touch me, she begged. *Do something to show you love me.*

"I just don't feel like socializing," was his reply. "But I think we should go and see her, so she won't feel neglected."

I feel neglected.

She took his hand and felt a slight jerk, as though his first reaction was to withdraw.

"What else do you want to do on your vacation?" She would keep it neutral and hope he would make the next move.

"I don't know. What's wrong with just hanging around home?"

"That doesn't seem very special to me, but it's your vacation. I just thought we should do something to entertain Mary Ellen. We could go swimming, I guess. Take a picnic to Bear Mountain. Visit some of those old houses, the Van Cortlandt Manor in Croton, the Philipse farm. Things like that."

He chuckled. "That doesn't sound much like Mary Ellen."

"No, I guess not." She had been thinking more of Gail, who loved the old restorations, with their guides in Colonial costume.

She moved his hand to her breast, which was shielded behind her nightgown and the sheet. He pulled away as though she had burned him.

"Carl," she said, "it's all right."

"You haven't seen the doctor yet," he reminded her. "You told me you had to see the doctor first, and get his O.K. stamp. Where do you think he'll stamp you?" He began to prod her abdomen through the sheet. It tickled. She doubled over onto her side.

"I didn't mean we had to go all the way. Not right now."

"You need your sleep," he said, getting up from the bed. "I'll be along in a while."

He left the room, closing the door behind him. She lay alone in the stifling darkness, and felt empty.

13

The telephone rang while she was in the basement unloading the washing machine. Why not an extension in the basement? she wondered as she stumbled up the backless stairs.

It was Barbara.

"Hi, Joyce, how's it going? I hope you're keeping my kid on a leash." She sounded grim.

"As best I can." Good grief, had she already heard about Mary Ellen's escapade?

"She's more of a woman than I thought," Joyce went on, hoping to avert further talk about Mary Ellen's wandering. "She got what she calls 'it' yesterday, just when we were swimming. And Carl keeps bugging her about her clothes. It seems to bother him. Would you mind if she and I went shopping for some bras?"

"Bras? Did she ask for bras? That's a new one."

"No, but I thought—"

"Oh, you mean because of Carl. That's something we don't have to cope with here."

"I think it's because of the murders. He doesn't want her—you know—conspicuous."

"Oh, that bothers him, does it? Well, okay. As long as she wants it. It's just something that never came up. They're not the status symbol they used to be. What do you hear about the latest?"

"Nothing. Only a rumor that it's the other missing girl."

"I don't mean *that* latest. I mean the *latest*. Joyce, you really ought to keep in touch with the world. It's your world. Haven't you heard there's another one missing?"

"Since when?" Oh, God, and Mary Ellen was out. It could have been Mary Ellen.

"This one might be different. The girl's twenty-one years

old, but under the circumstances, her parents are pretty worried. They say she's not the sort of person who would just go off."

"That's what all parents say." Even to her own ears, it sounded like feeble reassurance. "Where did you hear this?"

"On my favorite news station. Like I say, Joyce, you ought to keep in touch. This isn't happening in Pakistan, it's right where you are."

She did not like being lectured, even if Barbara was older and wiser.

"Probably a case of media hype. If I hear anything, I'll let you know."

Gail came into the kitchen and sat down at the table.

"I believe you conjectured the other two were a case of Greenwich Village," Barbara reminded her.

"Well . . ." She did not want to talk about it, now that Gail was here. "Everybody in this house is—" She fumbled for a metaphor that Barbara had not used, "on a very tight rein."

Silently Gail measured her half-bowl of cold cereal. Joyce nodded toward the grapefruit that sat by her place. Instead of eating, Gail watched her.

Barbara's voice came clearly over the wire. "I'd almost be inclined to bring her home, except I have a vacation coming up and I do want to get away. It's the only thing that keeps me sane for the rest of the year. I always sent her to camp before, but she refused to go this year. Hates the regimentation. So hang onto her, will you? Remind her about strange men. Is she up yet?"

"No, still sleeping. Want me to get her?"

"God, no. She's vile when she first wakes up. Okay, Joyce. My life is in your hands."

On impulse, before she could hang up, Joyce put in, "Carl's taking his own vacation in a couple of weeks, so maybe it'll be livelier here."

"Oh?"

"You know, more things to do. More people around. But we're sort of tied down with the baby."

"Yeah," Barbara breathed. Then, with a brisk "Okay," ended the conversation.

Gail's cereal was growing soggy as she listened. "Was

that Barbara? What did she say? Did somebody else get killed?"

"No, darling. Eat your breakfast."

"Well, what?"

She would hear it anyway, as Chief D'Amico had pointed out.

"Another girl is missing. But she's a grown-up girl, a woman, really. I'm sure nothing happened."

Gail's eyes grew huge. "How do you know nothing happened?"

"Because it's just . . . too much."

Which was no reason at all, and Gail knew it. Joyce left her dawdling over her cereal and went back down to the laundry. The spin was just about to finish. As she waited for it, a phrase of Barbara's came back to her. *My life is in your hands.*

My life? Did she mean that about Mary Ellen? Of course Mary Ellen was all she had. Any mother would feel that way. Joyce had not thought of Barbara as "any" mother, but perhaps she was.

The washer ceased its wild dance and she transferred the clothes to the dryer. In this weather nobody ever wore the same thing twice, and there were mountains of laundry. At least the basement was pleasantly cool, but those stairs, after a few dozen trips, could wear a person out.

When she went back up to the kitchen, Gail was still sitting at the table, staring at her half-eaten grapefruit.

"What's the matter, don't you want that?" Joyce asked. "I thought you liked grapefruit."

"I don't feel like eating right now. Mommy, I can't stop thinking about Valerie Cruz."

"Are you sick?"

Gail shook her head. Something had happened to her. This suddenly uneaten grapefruit was only a symptom. Damn Barbara for calling. But Barbara had a daughter, too. You couldn't blame her.

She thought of the mothers of the girls who had been murdered. She could understand the parents of even the missing twenty-one-year-old.

Oh, just damn it.

Why do people have to be crazy? Why couldn't they

catch a nut like that through some screening process back in grade school, and lock him up?

"Mommy, are you mad?"

Mad at Gail for not eating a grapefruit?

She put her arm around Gail's shoulder and drew her close. "I'm just so sorry this summer is ruined for you, honey. For all of us."

They both jumped at the sound of the doorbell. It was Anita.

"Hi, can I come in?"

"Of course, Anita." Would the child never leave them alone? "You didn't walk again, did you? I don't think it's a good idea."

"Don't worry, I don't talk to anybody. Did you know there's another girl missing?"

"That's exactly why I think you shouldn't go around by yourself. Really, Anita."

The girl tossed her long hair. "My mother doesn't care."

"I'll bet she does. She's really quite worried about those murders."

Mary Ellen came sleepily down the stairs, wearing a short, spaghetti-strapped nightgown.

"Joyce, Adam's awake, and he's fussing. Shall I take care of him? Is it time for his bath?"

"You eat your breakfast, dear. I'll call you when it's bath time." Joyce went upstairs and found that Adam had made a mess of himself. She was glad Mary Ellen had not seen it. In flushing the disposable diaper, she managed to clog the toilet. It stopped just short of overflowing.

This is not my day, she said to herself. They had a plunger somewhere. In the basement, probably, of all dumb places. Any instrument specifically designed for de-clogging toilets ought to be kept near the toilet. She missed apartment living, all on one level.

As she approached the kitchen, she heard Anita's voice, low and urgent.

"Come on. If I don't get them back, somebody's going to steal them, and then Denise'll kill me. Come on, Mary Ellen, Gail's a scaredy chicken, but you're not."

Joyce barely glanced at them as she passed by. It was something clandestine. She did not trust Anita, who could do as she liked, but please leave Gail and Mary Ellen out of it.

At the foot of the stairs she turned on a light. The far end of the basement depressed her. There was the oil burner with its many arms, like a giant octopus; the long unused coal bin which Carl had covered to keep away dirt and drafts, and two old upholstered chairs they wanted to get rid of, but the sanitation people would not pick up furniture.

On the work table, which Carl seldom used, lay a small stack of newspapers. Good for him, he must have been collecting them for recycling. Perhaps she ought to save bottles and aluminum cans as well.

She found the plunger and went back upstairs. They were grouped around the kitchen table like three statues, waiting for her to get out of earshot.

She stopped and confronted them. A ridiculous confrontation, with the plunger in her hand.

"Now listen. Nobody'd better do anything funny, understand? This is serious. If you have to disobey your parents, choose some way where you won't get hurt. Just remember, once you're dead, you're dead forever."

She stood for a moment, watching them. They stared back at her. Perhaps she had guessed wrong. But they weren't laughing, so maybe she hadn't. With an almost imperceptible nod, like an exclamation point, she left them and continued upstairs. At least they would know she was keeping an eye on them.

Mary Ellen came flitting up after her, to help with Adam's bath. Neither mentioned the scene in the kitchen. Joyce did not want to destroy the false impression that she had known what they were talking about.

In the middle of the bath, the telephone rang.

"Déjà vu!" exclaimed Mary Ellen. "I hope it's not my mother again."

"Your mother already called this morning."

It was Sheila. "Oh, God, Joyce, is Anita over there? Please say she is. No, I mean tell the truth if she isn't."

"She really is," said Joyce. "And she walked around by the road, if that's any consolation."

"Oh, thank God. Just keep her there, will you? I don't even want her going on the road by herself. She might accept a ride from somebody, and my God, *we* don't know who it is. It could be somebody from around here. Someone she'd know."

"You don't think it's Mr. Lattimer?" Joyce asked.

"Well, we don't know, do we? I still can't understand why they don't bring him in, but we don't know."

"Sheila, I'm in the middle of giving Adam his bath."

"Oh, my God, you're not going to let him drown!"

"No, Mary Ellen's there. I'll keep—"

"Do you know there's another girl gone? That's the third already. Do you wonder I'm jumpy? My cousin Herb, on the police force, he says people have actually been threatening them."

"Threatening the police?"

"Because they haven't found the guy. Well, I told him I don't wonder. Here I am with three daughters—"

"What good does it do to threaten the police?"

"Oh, you know. I didn't say it made sense, I just said— Joyce, how can you be so calm? You're right in the middle of it."

"I am?"

"You're so close to the woods. Actually I guess we are, too, except there're some houses between us and it. All you have is that meadow."

"Sheila, I've got to get back to Adam. I'll keep an eye on Anita. She's still around, I can hear her voice."

She returned to the bathroom to find that Mary Ellen had finished rising Adam, had wrapped him in a towel, and was sitting on the edge of the bathtub, crooning to him.

Joyce cleaned and put away the bathinette. She felt strangely hollow. Or perhaps as though she were split in two, one of her with the surface calm that Sheila had noted, and the other with a strange, not quite physical pounding deep inside. As if something were knocking to come in. Something unspeakable, which she could not admit. She remembered that her grandmother had sometimes had premonitions.

Instantly she closed her mind to it. As though, by denying, she could keep it from happening.

14

The next morning she left her children at Sheila's house, an arrangement to which Mary Ellen consented only because Denise and fourteen-year-old June were there, and went to see her doctor. The six weeks were over, the significance of which had eluded Carl. Adam was six weeks old and his mother's body, after childbirth, had returned to normal. Everything should have been all right with the world.

It *is* all right, she tried to convince herself as she drove back through the village an hour later. The doctor had said everything was fine.

It was—except that in front of the police station, cars were parked that had press cards on their dashboards.

She slowed instinctively as an ambulance sped toward her, gliding like a ghost with no lights or siren. Her heartbeat quickened. It had come from the hill where she, and the Farands, lived.

The children! But there had been no lights, no siren. It was not an emergency.

The hill. The woods. No, not the third girl.

In the car that followed it, she saw Chief D'Amico.

So it was. The third girl.

Still, she pressed the accelerator to reach Sheila's house as quickly as possible, just in case. But everything there was calm.

She did not mention the ambulance. She was sick of the whole thing, of Anita's excitement, Sheila's voluble alarm, Gail's pale silence. They would find out anyway. It would be in the papers, on the radio and television. The press was all over Cedarville.

She soon discovered to what extent it was all over Cedarville.

Anita greeted her by jumping up and down. "Guess what! A man came from the newspaper and he asked me about when I found the body. I'm going to be in the newspaper!"

Mary Ellen said, "But Gail found the body, too, and you didn't even tell him that."

"She did not. I found it, and then I told her."

"That's true," Joyce said, relieved that they had not pestered Gail with questions.

Anita followed them out to the car. "Can Gail and Mary Ellen sleep over?"

From Gail came an indrawn breath and a quick, secret shake of the head.

Joyce glanced at Mary Ellen, who was staring into space. "I'm afraid not, honey. I need them at home to help me."

Sheila pulled Anita away from the car. "I know how you feel," she told Joyce in a hushed tone that promised more discussion of the murders.

With a smile, Joyce cut her short. "I do need their help. Mary Ellen's just marvelous with the baby, and Gail likes to cook sometimes. I could put my feet up and relax, except I'd feel guilty." Quickly she got into the car and closed the door. She would pretend nothing was happening. For Gail's sake, and her own. She waved good-bye to Sheila, who had both hands clamped on a struggling Anita, and drove away.

She could not escape it for long. In the quiet afternoon, just after the grandfather clock had chimed two, a tan car with an elaborate radio antenna came up the driveway. She thought it might be the police again, but the young man who knocked at her kitchen door was someone she did not know.

He flashed a card at her. She could not see what it said.

"Ma'am, I understand your daughter was one of the kids who found the first body. Is she here? Could I talk to her for a minute?"

It ended in a plea. Joyce's face had frozen.

"Who are you?" she demanded.

"From the *News Item*." He took out his card again and held it while she read every word.

"I'm afraid not." She hoped Gail was in the house and

not outside where he might find her. "She's been very upset by this whole thing, and she wouldn't want to talk about it."

"You're speaking for her, ma'am. Could I have her opinion on that?"

"You could not. I'm her mother and I know how she feels. You won't get anything from her anyway. She didn't see a thing. Now please go."

"Just for a minute. Just a—"

"No! I said no! I don't give a damn about the public's right to information, or about your career. I care about my child, and if I have to get violent, I will."

She stood glaring at him. He was young and thin with an air of sincerity, but also the brashness of someone determined to get a news story. He bowed his head in mock capitulation, then stood away from the house and looked up at the second-story windows. Apparently seeing nothing, he returned to his car.

"I'll be back," he promised as he drove away.

He had gone only a short distance down the driveway when he had to stop for another car coming in.

This time it was the police. The reporter had to back up to let them enter the parking area, and then once again he drove off.

She felt an odd anticipation as Chief D'Amico got out of the car. This was something familiar, something reassuringly secure.

He had a partner with him, a young man with very curly blond hair that made her think of soap bubbles. D'Amico introduced him as Art Finneran.

"I'm glad you came," she told them. "Do I have any legal protection against reporters? That man who just left was hell-bent on bothering my daughter, and I don't think she can take much more of this."

"There's nothing that says you have to talk to them," D'Amico replied.

"I didn't. You found that girl, didn't you? The one who was missing the other day? I saw an ambulance."

"We found her." He sounded grim and yet resigned. "We're going around the neighborhood, asking if anybody noticed anything unusual that night. It doesn't have to seem related. Just anything different from the ordinary."

"Which night?" She could not remember when the girl had disappeared.

"Monday. She never came home from work that night—she worked in the city—but obviously she got back to Cedarville."

"Monday. That was the night my stepdaughter was out. Found a boyfriend and went out on his motorcycle without telling me. I was so worried I wouldn't have noticed an earthquake." She went on to describe the evening. It had been unusual, but only for the Gilwood family.

"Why don't you come inside?" she suggested. "It's cooler in the house. I usually close the blinds on days like this."

They followed her in and sat at the kitchen table, where the girls could not hear them. She offered them iced tea, which they declined.

D'Amico set his cap upside down on the table and twirled it slowly as he talked. "Mrs. Gilwood, how well do you know the neighbors?"

Her head jerked upright at his question. "Not very well. You get to know people who have children the same age as your children. They aren't the closest neighbors, but you know, the Farands—"

"Yes, I know them."

"Her cousin is one of your men."

"Right. So you haven't had much to do with anybody except the Farands?"

"And Bruce and Pam Cheskill."

"Nobody, for instance, on this road?"

"No, they're all older, or their children are older. Why do you want to know? It can't be—"

"In a very close-knit community," he said, "where everyone knows everyone else, and feels responsible for them, a thing like this—if it happened at all, you'd get to the bottom of it much faster. That's all. We have to try every possibility."

It sounded like an evasion. He must suspect someone, and wanted to find out more about him. Someone—on Shadowbrook Road? She could not believe it, even though she didn't know any of them very well.

"Every possibility," he said again, as though he could read her mind. He asked other questions, trying to bring out what she did know about her neighbors. He asked her about her own household.

"So you're mostly here alone with the children. What time does your husband get home from work?"

"Six-thirty. He takes a train that leaves Grand Central at five twenty-three."

"Is he ever late?"

"When the train's late."

"Ever work late? Take a later train?"

"Of course, now and then. Everybody does things differently sometimes. What are you driving at? What is it you want to know?"

She fought a mad urge to get up and open a window. She was suffocating, but the window would only make it hotter.

"I want to know everything I can," he said gently. "Then we start putting it together. And only after we've gotten somewhere can we sort out what's relevant and what isn't, so bear with us, okay?"

"Yes, I'm sorry. I didn't— It just sounded—"

"We're asking everybody the same kind of question, if that makes you feel any better."

She was surprised to find that it did. "But I still don't like it. Do you really think it's somebody from around here?"

"Chances are, it isn't," he said. "It would have to be somebody awfully naive—or pretty damn clever—to commit that kind of mayhem in a place where he's known and recognized, and expect to get away with it."

"If he thinks at all," put in Finneran.

At D'Amico's request she went to find Mary Ellen, so they could ask her if she had seen anything noteworthy while riding around on David's motorcycle.

Boy crazy, Joyce thought as Mary Ellen's eyes widened at the sight of the youthful Art Finneran. No, she hadn't seen anything. She had been on the back roads halfway to Peekskill, and they had stopped for frozen yoghurt someplace way out in the country, but she couldn't say where. She spoke breathlessly, more to Art Finneran, who silently jotted a few notes, than to D'Amico, who was questioning her. Finally they dismissed her, but she remained in the kitchen. The policemen rose to leave.

"Thanks, ladies," D'Amico said with a weary smile. "We'll try the other people around here, and hope this guy might have made at least one slip somewhere."

"I wish I could help you," Joyce said.

"Not your fault. The guy just doesn't want to be caught, and so far he's been smart enough, or lucky enough, not to leave any traces."

"But he must be insane," she said. "Mustn't he? To do all those things? Would he even think about being caught?"

"He may, in the long run, want to be caught," D'Amico replied "even though he doesn't know it, and that's why he keeps doing this. But he can't recognize that. It's all part of it."

"It doesn't make sense."

"Of course it doesn't make sense. We're dealing with an irrational mind. In his own twisted way, though, it makes sense to him. This could be his release. His safety valve. The rest of the time he could be walking around looking as normal as the rest of us."

"Really? Then it could be—anybody."

"I wouldn't say anybody. I've got my doubts it could be you, for instance. And I'm pretty sure it isn't me."

"Are you saying the person might not know himself?"

"That's possible, Or if he does, he wouldn't see it the way we do. He may even know it's against the law, but to him it isn't wrong. Or if it's wrong, it's still something he has to do, you know what I mean?"

After they left, Mary Ellen sighed. "Did you see him?" As though Joyce might not have. "Isn't he cute? All that curly hair, and I just love uniforms. It makes people look so—capable."

"A little young for my taste," said Joyce. "If I had to choose, I'd take D'Amico. He's a real man."

"Who, the old one?"

"Old? I doubt if he's forty." She took a breath to say something more. To tell Mary Ellen, Please don't be so boy crazy that you get carried away with the wrong person. But to start lecturing would only make Mary Ellen stubborn.

With the police coming right on his heels, she had almost forgotten about the reporter. By the time Carl came home she was thinking of it again, and had worked herself into a state of pique. Almost triumphantly she related how she had chased him away.

"We really ought to get a dog, Carl, there's too much going on here, and this house is so isolated. I'd feel a lot safer."

He was unpacking his briefcase, taking out all three daily papers, the *Times*, the *News*, and the *Post*.

"I suppose I never told you," he said, "I'm allergic to dogs."

No, he hadn't told her. The subject had never come up, and his bland statement made her feel oddly deflated.

"Well, then, maybe a Pinkerton guard." She started toward the stairs to remind the girls about setting the table.

He called her back. "Did you see this in the paper?"

She approached it with dread, for she caught a glimpse of a photograph. But it was only the site where the third girl had been found, not the body itself. Below it were three smiling portraits: the victims. *What if somebody came to the door and asked for a picture of my daughter?*

He motioned her to sit down and read it with him.

"Later," she said. "I've got dinner almost ready."

With a final, questioning look, he laid the papers on the sofa and went up to take his shower. When they gathered at the dinner table, he was silent at first, apparently disappointed that she had not shared his fascination with the murder story. She hoped he would not talk about it in front of the girls, and felt relieved when he did not talk much at all.

After the meal was over, the dishes cleared away, and the children watching television, she picked up the paper. Carl gave her an approving glance across the sofa. It was the excitement that got to him, she supposed. The mood of crisis. He wanted to share it.

The victim was a girl named Toni Lemich. She had a round face, short dark hair worn like a cap, and heavily outlined eyes.

Joyce skimmed the columns. It was disgusting the way the newspapers latched onto these things. Like vultures.

Carl moved over beside her and pointed to a block of print set apart.

"Look, did you see that? A letter. The man wrote a letter to the paper."

"The murderer? Why can't they catch him from that?" For some reason she had never pictured the killer as an actual person, with the ability to get up in the morning, dress, buy groceries, or write a letter like anybody else.

Carl looked at her with a slight frown.

"How could they catch him? The letter was typed. It says so."

"I read somewhere that even a typewriter has its individual quirks," she said, "and they can identify it almost like handwriting."

He shrugged. "I don't know. Maybe with a manual you can. Even then, you'd have to start with a suspect. But I doubt they can identify something like an IBM, with that type ball. There must be millions of them in use. You can change the typeface, and the print's too even to have individual quirks."

"Did he do it on an IBM? I should think even that would narrow it down, at least to somebody who had access to one."

"Millions of people have access to them. Go on. Read it."

Dear Sirs,
    The Cedarville police are too slow. They don't even start to get warm yet. So in the meantime we have three cold bodies, maybe more to come, ha ha. Its getting to be a habit. Theres never any shortage of girls. When I want one I can always get one.

                                    Your friend
                                The Cedarville Slasher

"What do you think?" Carl asked.

She closed her eyes. "I think it's obscene."

"Obscene? How?"

"Carl, really, how can you be like that? Don't you think of these girls as people?"

"Of course. But how is my thinking of them as people going to change anything?"

She didn't like this. Not at all. It wasn't Carl. She turned back to the paper, if only to avoid talking to him.

There were two articles, one a straight news story about the Lemich murder, the other an analysis of the crimes to date. All three murders, it quoted the police as saying, were undoubtedly linked. And all were obviously sex crimes, although only in the third case were they able to establish that the victim had been molested.

They had called in a psychiatrist to try to analyze the murders and the murderer.

This was clearly a man with sexual problems, Dr. Ronald K. Ballard stated. Possibly a man in his thirties or forties, plagued with fears of impotence or homosexuality, or with occupational or marital problems leading to a loss of self-esteem. He could overcome his impotence with sudden attacks on women.

A paranoid personality with deep explosive urges. Where did they come from? He may have felt betrayed at some time in his past by an important female figure. In cases like this it was most often the mother—desertion or remarriage—but from the ages of the victims, the possibility of someone younger could not be ruled out.

The murderer, the article continued, was probably an ordinary member of the community, undetected because he carried a veneer of social acceptability—a job, a nice home, may even have been married.

Could be functioning on two levels. Possibly a split personality, but Dr. Ballard doubted it. The murderer, he thought, knew what he was doing.

She felt too sick to read about the finding of the body. That deep internal pounding had started again. She wondered how she had ever passed the doctor's exam, even though it was not exactly her heart, it was something deeper and even more fundamental. Her life, perhaps.

She looked around the living room at her home, her shelter, where everything was normal. The girls sat in the television corner, giggling at some comedy. The lamplight cast a warm glow over the room, but outside those black windows, somebody could be watching.

Carl was not there. While she was reading, he had gotten up and left. The kitchen door was closed. Faintly, through the sound from the television, she could hear his voice.

She pushed open the swinging door and went into the kitchen. It was dark, but she could see him sitting at the table. She reached for the light switch. He caught her wrist. His grip was steel, implacable. Then it dissolved and she thought it trembled a little before it released her, like the jelly of her own arms and legs.

He said into the telephone, "Yes, well, I just wanted to let you know I'm with you. I won't bother you anymore now. Good-bye."

She heard the click as he hung up. Her eyes were adjusting to the darkness. She saw him take a handkerchief from his pocket and mop his face.

"What was that?" she asked.

"Why do you come barging in here when I'm on the phone?"

"I didn't know you were on the phone. I heard your voice, and I thought it might be the police, or another reporter."

"Police?"

"They came today, right after the reporter. To ask if we'd seen anything. You know, because all the bodies were found near here. I'm sorry I interrupted."

"It was a private phone call."

"I'm really sorry." She edged toward the door.

This time he caught her with his voice.

"You know, I knew that girl."

"You did?"

"We used to ride the same train out from the city. I didn't know her very well. Just the same face night after night. A few words now and then. I think I sat next to her once."

Joyce waited, letting him speak.

Finally he said, "I was calling her family. I thought I'd let them know they've got a friend."

"That was nice, Carl. I'd be afraid to call somebody who just—you know."

"Why be afraid?"

"I'd just be afraid to call. I even hate writing notes.

You'd think I'd be used to it, after it happened to me. She gave the door a gentle push.

"Sit down, why don't you?" he said.

"Can I turn on the light?"

"What for? It's cooler without it."

"It'd be cooler if you didn't have the door closed."

"All right, then, open it."

She pushed open the door and joined him at the table. Light and sound flowed in from the living room, but it flowed past them and did not disturb them.

"I can't help wondering what happened to her," he said.

"Is that what you wanted to talk about?"

"I saw her get off the train and start walking. She only lived a few blocks from the station, but she had to walk along River Street, and it's pretty lonely there."

"And it was late," Joyce said. Odd that they should both have been late, both on the same train. Something went *bump* inside her, and she wondered for a moment whether Toni Lemich could have been more to him than just someone he saw on the train.

She almost asked. And stopped herself. He hadn't seemed to notice her remark.

"I worried about her sometimes," he went on. "I thought of giving her a ride home."

"Maybe you should have."

Why hadn't he? It would have been natural. Unless he wanted to avoid being seen with her.

"I offered. She said she'd be all right."

"But she wasn't. Maybe—somebody else—"

He shrugged. "We'll never know."

"I should hope we'll know. I hope they catch that creep, and damn quick. You don't realize what this is doing to us. To the girls, and me, and Sheila— To everybody, I guess."

"You're afraid?"

"What do you think? Especially here, in this house that nobody can even see."

"What do you mean, nobody can see?"

"It's hidden. Nobody else can see this house. Remember, we thought that was lovely when we bought it, but now I wish we lived in a nice cozy development with the neighbors squeezed in on both sides."

"She lived in a house like that. It didn't help her."

"Toni Lemich?"

"You know, when I think of her all tied up like that—"

"Carl, stop!" A wave of something passed over her, nausea and something worse—fear.

"How do you know she was tied up?"

"It says so in the paper. Didn't you read the paper? Didn't you read how—"

"*Stop.* I don't want to talk about it, ever. I don't want to know."

He stared at her for a moment. Then he said, "You're an ostrich, darling. "

It was a hollow "darling," almost as meaningless as Larry's show-business endearments, but it was a step in some sort of direction.

Encouraged, she said, "I saw the doctor today. My six-week checkup, remember? I'm all back to normal."

She waited for him to respond. She wondered if he had even heard her.

"You'll find out," she said, "if we can pry those kids away from the television and get them to bed."

But later, when the television was off and the house silent, and she slipped into bed beside him, he lay with his back to her. She reached out and touched him, running her fingers along his side, under the arm. She could almost feel him shrink away from her.

The room was hot and close, except for a breeze from the electric fan on the dresser.

"Carl?"

"Mm?" he grunted.

"I'm here."

"Go to sleep."

She propped herself on her elbow. "What's the matter? It's been almost a year."

He half turned his head. "Sshh, do you want the kids to wake up?"

"They can't hear, the doors are all closed. And anyway, they must know. They know where Adam came from."

His head returned to the pillow. She waited for some response. He ignored her.

She reached out again. "Carl, what's wrong?"

Again he seemed to shrivel under her touch. She pulled back her hand. It was as though she repelled him.

Perhaps . . . those evenings coming home with Toni Lemich . . . Maybe there was something there.

"Listen," she whispered, "aren't you ever going to— I mean—"

"Not now. Just not now. Go to sleep."

He was unnatural. Larry had always wanted her, even when she knew he had others. She began to feel ashamed of herself, pleading like this.

For a while she lay in the dark, with tears just behind her eyes. It wasn't that she was horny. It was the closeness she wanted, the love between the two of them. They had created a baby together. They had a family, a home. There should have been love.

She moved closer to him, so that her voice would fall into his ear, even thought he might be drifting off to sleep. But he wasn't. She could still feel the tension.

"Carl—honey—is something wrong? Just tell me. Something you might be afraid of, or worried about?"

"What are you talking about?"

"I just want you to know that you can be free with me. I know some men worry if they think, you know, they're not going to make it. They think the woman's going to laugh at them, or get angry. They don't want to try."

Perhaps he was influenced by that newspaper article, about the killer who might have a problem with impotence. Surely Carl would not identify with that. But it might play into a fundamental fear.

He said, "That's too ridiculous for words."

Was it really another woman? She hadn't taken the idea seriously before.

"Is there somebody else?" she asked, and was amazed at how calmly she managed it.

"Joyce, go to sleep."

Not "darling" this time, nor "sweetheart." Just Joyce.

"You're in love with somebody else, aren't you?"

"I'm not in love with anybody," he told her angrily.

She nodded sadly to herself, thinking that he may have spoken the truth without meaning to. *Not in love with anybody.*

Still, to her way of thinking, a man was not like that.

He never rejected a woman just because he didn't love her. She went back to her original idea.

"You know, it could be just a little thing. Have you thought of seeing a doctor?"

He turned to her with such vehemence that his elbow jabbed into her rib.

"What the hell do I need a doctor for? What are you talking about? Why don't you shut up and go to sleep?"

"I just thought—"

No, she couldn't talk to him now, he was too angry. She expected him to get up and leave the bed. He simply lay as he had been, facing away from her.

She lowered her head to the pillow and closed her eyes.

After a while he said, through clenched teeth, "Don't need a doctor."

She forced herself to answer. "I didn't say you need one. But sometimes if you're worried about something, and you go to a doctor and they tell you you're all right, it helps you feel better."

"Saw a doctor," he muttered. "Ages ago. Nothing but talk. Can't fix anything talking. He didn't make her come back."

Barbara?

"It was her fault," he went on. "She forgot about me. All those damn— I went looking for her. Couldn't —couldn't—"

He turned his head slightly. In the dim earthlight, she saw that his eyes were closed.

"Forgot about me, God damn you. Whaddaya expect? Go strutting around with your tits, wagging your ass for the boys. A goddamn whore."

Barbara?

Or me?

"Carl—"

"Shut up, bitch, I don't want to hear it. Don't—talk—me—grow up. Goddamn boys. I hate you, shut up."

She almost thought she saw a tear on his cheek, but he flung himself away, his back to her again, and lay like a block of steel.

She dared not move. It might set him off. He might— He hated her.

But why? What had she done?

Unless—

Not her. But who? Barbara? Olivia? Daniella?

Daniella . . .

Daniella . . .

She stared at the ceiling. The room was pale gray, shadowy, as though the darkness was something she could touch. The fan blew across her with fingers of wind. Next to her, in his crib, Adam made a small sniffing noise as he slept.

She stared at the ceiling and wondered, What do I do now?

15

During the night she dreamed about Larry. It seemed as though she was back in that basement apartment on Bleecker Street and all that had happened afterwards was a fantasy.

She woke slowly, with Larry breathing beside her. She could feel his warmth, feel where his weight depressed the mattress. She had no thought but that it was Larry, until she opened her eyes and saw the room. Not quite right, this room. She had seen it before, but . . .

Her confusion lasted only a moment, then seemed to peel off and fall away. Last night came clearly back and she felt cold, although the sun was up and the day already warm.

Adam was beginning to stir. She slipped out of bed without disturbing Carl. Through the open window she could see the meadow, glistening clean in the early morning light and alive with the singing of birds.

She lifted Adam from his crib. The clock radio on the nighttable gave a little pop and began to play softly. Carl sat up. He looked at her, standing beside the bed with the baby in her arms, and gave her a wry-comic smile.

"Another day, another dime," he said.

She managed to smile back. It's all right, she told herself. It's all right.

By the time she had finished feeding Adam and joined Carl downstairs, he was already eating breakfast. He made a gesture of pushing out her chair so she could sit down. Her familiar Carl. Nothing remained of last night, not even a memory. Perhaps he had only been tired. Or she had misunderstood.

That telephone call to the Lemich family. It was sweet of him.

But something still nagged at her. Something she could not identify and didn't want to think about.

"So you want to go somewhere on my vacation?" he asked.

"It's not important. Whatever you want."

"Maybe a short trip. It just seems like such a hassle, with the kid."

"It is a hassle. I was thinking of the girls. But they're all right. Some people would consider this a vacation, out here in the country."

"As long as they don't have to go to school," he agreed. "That's vacation enough."

He kissed her good-bye when he left. *Tonight?* she wanted to ask, but kept her silence.

She was loading the dishwasher when Sheila called.

"Got a minute?"

"Special for you," said Joyce. "Otherwise I don't 'got a minute.' What are you doing up so early?"

"You mean what am I doing on the telephone so early. I'm always up. It's about tonight. We're having this meeting and I have to call about a thousand people, starting with you."

A sort of town meeting, she went on to explain. With the police.

"To talk about this thing. The police are really getting it rough. You know, if you don't pick up a lead, you don't, but the whole village is on their backs. Well, you'd think they could come up with something. Look, now I'm doing it myself, and I know what they're going through. But I know what the rest of us are going through, too."

"So you want me to come."

"Don't you want to? Don't you care about getting at this thing before it gets us?"

"I—guess so."

"What I hate is not being able to do anything," Sheila went on. "At least this is something. And the police are going to give us some tips on keeping safe. Do you want Foster and me to pick you up? Around seven-thirty? It starts at eight."

Again that odd, overdone heartbeat. She did not know why. Some premonition. She didn't want to leave her home.

"I don't know. The children—"

"For God's sake, leave them with Carl. Unless he wants to go, too. You could bring them all over here. I think June is old enough, and Denise and Mary Ellen, as long as they bolt all the doors."

"I really don't think Carl would be interested. And he's not—I mean—sometimes he has to work late."

"Why don't you call him? Find out if he'll be home. Bring the kids over here and we can all go together."

"Okay, I'll let you know."

She was relieved to have put it off. Maybe she could think of something. It wasn't that she didn't want to help. It was—She didn't know. The children, perhaps. She didn't even want to leave them with Carl. She wanted them where she could see them.

And what difference would it make whether she did or did not go to the meeting? She couldn't help them. The police were doing all they could. Sooner or later they would break through. It had happened with those other freaks, the Son of Sam, the Boston Strangler, Charlie Chopoff . . .

Crazy people. All of them. Really out of it, at least some of the time.

Yet someone must have known. Someone close to them must have known how crazy they were, but perhaps they thought . . .

Well, you just wouldn't ever think it, when it's someone you know. It doesn't seem possible.

No, she thought, I don't mean that. Not about *me*. Just because a person had a childhood trauma. And not even a serious one at that.

She refused to think about it. It was ridiculous. She would know, if there was anything worth thinking about.

She did not call Carl. He disliked being bothered at the office, and when he came home she was glad she hadn't. He was in one of his silent moods.

"Dinner's all ready, so don't be long," she told him as he started upstairs. "I have to go to a meeting."

He grunted an answer. The phone rang and it was Sheila, wanting to know what her plans were. She felt as though Sheila were trapping her. She really wanted to stay home with her children.

"I don't know. I have sort of a headache."

"Take an aspirin. This is important. We'll be there at seven-thirty."

"Wait a minute, let me ask Carl."

He had just gone into the bathroom, but not yet turned on the shower. Quickly she explained about the meeting. Would he want to go, or would he look after the kids?

Instantly Gail came out of her room, her face stricken with anxiety. Mary Ellen looked up from the floor of her own room, where she lay writing another letter.

"Hell, no," Carl replied. "I've had a full day already. Think I want to go and listen to a bunch of idiots shooting off their mouths? Leave the kids, leave the dishes. The kids'll take care of everything."

"You hope."

She finished her phone call and served the dinner. As they took their places at the table, Mary Ellen, with a quick glance at her father, asked, "Why can't I go to that meeting?"

Gail looked up hopefully. "Me, too."

"It's for grown-ups," said Joyce. "It can't last more than a couple of hours. And you'll be having a lovely time with the dishes."

Feeling uneasy, she sat down in the chair Carl pulled out for her. His manners were impeccable. But the girls—why were they so eager to go?

Maybe they thought it would be an adventure. She might have considered taking them—certainly they had a stake in it, too—except for what the meeting could disclose. There might be details they shouldn't hear.

"You're not eating," said Carl. "I thought you were in a big hurry."

"I am." She picked up her fork, but she wasn't really hungry.

She had changed her clothes before dinner. Adam was fed and sleeping. She was ready before the Farands came for her, and helped the girls clear the table, to distract herself from the odd feeling in her stomach. A feeling of nervous dread. She could not understand it.

"They're here, Mommy," Gail told her.

Both girls stood at the kitchen door to wave her off. She

might have been leaving for Siberia, for the size of the pang she felt.

"Do you always get a send-off like that?" Sheila asked.

"I don't usually go away like this. I guess it's a pretty big event."

The meeting was to be held in the high school auditorium. As they drew into the already crowded parking lot, she forgot her private panic, whatever the cause of it, and began to appreciate the community feeling all around her. There had never been anything like this in the big sprawling city. Or if there was, she had not had time for it.

They joined the throngs that swarmed into the auditorium. Not long after they arrived, all the seats became filled and latecomers had to stand.

On the stage was a row of chairs and a lectern with a microphone. At ten minutes past eight, five men and three women filed out to the chairs. She recognized Chief D'Amico. One of the men looked at his watch, stood up, and approached the lectern.

It was stuffy in the large room, even with the windows open and several large fans blowing from the wall.

Again for a moment she saw the two girls waving good-bye.

"Ladies and gentlemen," the first speaker began, "we have come here tonight for a very unpleasant reason, and I can see it's touched a lot of you. I have to admit, we never expected this much turnout."

A murmur went around the audience.

The man talked on, summarizing the crimes, and then introduced the mayor of Cedarville.

The mayor spoke even more emphatically about the horrors that gripped his village, and repeated the media phrase "reign of terror."

The first man rose again and introduced the Chief of Police, Frank D'Amico.

D'Amico spoke more concretely.

"The police can't be everywhere at one time, ladies and gentlemen. We're only a sixteen-man force and we're already working around the clock on this investigation." He held up his hand at the growls of protest.

"Mind you, I'm not trying to excuse the fact that we

haven't found the perpetrator yet. All I'm saying is we can't put a guard on every young girl and woman in the area. It's got to be up to the girls themselves and the parents to try to keep 'em safe.

"It's got to be emphasized to these girls," he continued, "that it's *never* safe to hitch a ride or go with somebody they don't know, or don't know well. It's only an elementary precaution never to go with a stranger, no matter what excuses, reasons, or even force he might use."

A woman shouted from the third row, "What if it isn't a stranger?"

"We've thought of that, too," D'Amico replied. "In a small community like this, it could very well be somebody they recognize. Only thing you can do is avoid going with anybody that's not your family. Not at a time like this."

The same woman shouted again, "What if he has a gun?"

"I was coming to that." D'Amico looked around the auditorium. "You know, ladies and gentlemen, we all get this picture of a guy stepping out, pointing a gun, and forcing a young lady into his car or whatever at gunpoint. If somebody pointed a gun at you, you'd probably do what he said, right? Now take another look at it. There's a lot of circumstances when that would be exactly the wrong thing to do.

"My advice to the girls, or anybody else in this situation, is, RUN. Sounds crazy, but that way you've at least got a chance.

"If you run, you're a moving target. It's not so easy to hit a moving target, especially with a small weapon like a handgun. There's a pretty good chance he's not an expert marksman. It's a terror weapon, for the most part. Chances are, he won't even fire. If he does, he probably can't hit you, or at least not fatally. Think about it."

D'Amico paused. Except for a few indignant murmurs, the auditorium was silent. He resumed his speech, concluding with instructions to remain in populated, well-lit areas, to be suspicious of any and everybody, and to report any untoward incidents to the police.

After pausing again to let it all sink in, he introduced the next speaker. "Dr. Ronald Ballard, who's going to give us some tips on what kind of a guy in all probability we're looking for. That's not to say we limit our search to this person, it only gives us a few guidelines. Ron?"

Dr. Ballard was a tall man with graying hair and a handlebar mustache. He began by repeating what D'Amico had just said: that his psychiatric profile was not intended to exclude other possibilities.

"We're dealing," he told the audience, "with a very clever person. A man with real cunning. If not, he'd have been caught by now. He could be a man with a very big contempt for society. He could be a man who's enjoying the publicity his crimes are getting, even if he has to remain anonymous.

"Or the whole thing could be a cry for help. With every crime he could be calling out, 'Catch me, catch me. Help me.'"

Joyce's throat began to ache with tension. She forced herself to relax, muscle by muscle, as she listened to what the psychiatrist had to say. It was not a very specific profile. It covered just about every possibility there was.

"His cleverness," Dr. Ballard continued, "suggests that our man is probably intelligent and educated. He's probably quite a presentable person, the way he can lure these girls to go with him. The fact that he seems to be an area resident makes it fairly likely he's a family man. He may even appear to have a good sexual adjustment, but underneath it all, there's something very wrong."

Very wrong . . . very wrong . . . It was wrong that it had to be someone like that, and not Mr. Lattimer, who would be so easy to detect. Maybe the psychiatrist was very wrong.

She heard phrases about hostility toward women. "His mother may have abandoned him in some way," Dr. Ballard said, "or may have seemed to abandon him."

But why take it out on innocent people? He'd have to be crazy to begin with, wouldn't he, for it to affect him like that?

She was barely aware that she had raised her hand, until the doctor nodded in her direction. For a moment she stared at him, amazed at being recognized, and then stood up.

"But why," she asked, "would he take it out by killing innocent people? It doesn't make sense. Wouldn't he have

to be crazy to begin with, to react like that? In the newspaper you said his mother might have remarried. Lots of
mothers remarry, and their children don't end up killing
people."

The doctor smiled patiently. "I said she may have
seemed to abandon him," he explained. "It's how the child
perceives a thing that determines his response to it. We
don't know what led up to his individual perception of the
problem. But to react so violently—yes, undoubtedly he's
someone with a weak ego. A poor ability to adjust. That,
too, may have been acquired through childhood influences.
Or, just as some people haven't a normal amount of physical stamina, and succumb more easily to physical illness,
some haven't a normal amount of emotional stamina."

"But why?" she asked.

"We don't know. It could be that sometime in the fu-
ture we'll be able to detect and help these people in time
to avert this kind of tragedy."

"But why all of a sudden? Why would he blow up all of
a sudden, right now?" She did not want to let him go. She
wanted to ask so much, but was not quite sure just what it
was she wanted to know.

"In a case like this," the doctor replied, "there's likely to
be some event that triggers the explosion. It could be an
event that seems very unimportant to anybody else, but it
makes some kind of meaningful connection in the killer's
own mind."

Gradually Joyce melted back into her seat, while the
doctor went on talking.

"The actions of a psychotic murderer may seem random
and senseless to the rest of us, but for him they make
sense, in terms of how he perceives things. Later he may
wonder why he did it. Or he may not actually see himself
as the one who did it. He may even be begging for help,
as I said before, but what he does is the only thing he *can*
do at that time."

Sheila was shaking her head. Joyce whispered, "I can't
understand it, either. I just can't understand somebody
being so out of control."

A man rose and asked, "Could it be a person with some
kind of fetish, like for dark hair or something?"

"No," shouted another voice, "the first girl was blond."

D'Amico, joining Dr. Ballard at the lectern, said, "I don't think there's any point in speculating on that sort of thing. I think there's only one factor that governed his selection of victims, and I think that factor is opportunity. The guy had to kill, he had to go through his gruesome ritual, and he happened to pick whoever he could find."

Gruesome ritual, Joyce repeated to herself as the questions and answers swirled about her. The only crazy person around was Mr. Lattimer. She could imagine him living a life of rituals, there in his shack with the summer fires and the junk-filled yard.

And Anita, that time she tried to drown Gail.

She turned her head so that she could just see Foster Farand on the other side of Sheila. His gray eyes looked out from behind steel-rimmed glasses, and his mouth was pursed attentively and rather engagingly as he listened. It couldn't be gentle Foster.

But Dr. Ballard had said "a man who fits into the community." Not Lattimer. It was a man you wouldn't suspect.

So it could be anybody . . . anybody . . . anybody . . .

No, impossible. It couldn't be just anybody. It couldn't be—anyone close to her. She would know. How could she not know?

But someone must know. She was back to that. Someone would be close enough—if it wasn't Lattimer. Someone knew and was lying. Protecting the killer.

She glanced at Sheila. At the other people around her. She tried to imagine how it would feel—knowing.

She heard someone scream, "No more handguns!" and looked up. D'Amico was talking again. He nodded in response to the comment but his reply was drowned in more shouting. A woman in a middle row jumped to her feet.

"What are you police doing here, anyway? Why aren't you out there catching that maniac?"

There were cries of agreement from the audience. Joyce felt stifled, pressed in by the heat and the rustling and stirring of the crowd.

Foster Farand stood up. "Let's not forget, people . . ."

The noise continued. D'Amico thundered into the microphone, "Quiet, please." In the startled lull that followed, Foster began again.

"Let's not forget, people, that this meeting was called by the community. The police and Dr. Ballard came as our invited guests. Chief D'Amico has given us sound advice based on his expertise, and I think we ought to respect that. We ought to respect the fact that the police have been running themselves ragged trying to solve the crimes. Have we been helping? We've got to remember it's a community problem, not just a police problem."

The same woman shouted, "Call the F.B.I."

Joyce whispered to Sheila, "I think I need some air. I'll be right outside. Don't worry about me, I'll wait by the car."

She felt as though everyone must be turning to stare as she slid out of her row and walked quickly up the aisle. When she looked back, they were paying no attention to her. The clamor rose. Someone called, "Get Lattimer!"

She walked faster. They were turning ugly. That was the trouble with bringing them all together. Their own impotence made them frustrated.

For a moment, as she stepped outside, a warm breeze blew, and then it was still again. Still and hot. With all the humidity, it scarcely cooled off at night. She looked toward the auditorium windows. The noise seemed to have died down. She could hear a single voice speaking.

She paced slowly on the sidewalk in front of the door. A locust tree cast a soft powdery shadow across the harsh lights of the parking lot. How silly of her to be out here alone. Mightn't the killer come around, just to watch the effect of the uproar he had caused?

But he couldn't do anything here. He would have to get her away, and she would not go. Even if he pointed a gun—

She jumped as a small door near what she supposed was the stage suddenly opened. A figure loomed in the dim light, and as the door closed behind it, sorted itself into Chief D'Amico.

He nodded briefly and started to walk on.

She ran after him. "Mr. D'Amico!"

He turned around so quickly she almost expected him to reach for a gun.

"How are you, ma'am? What are you doing out here?"

"I—it got too hot inside."

"Aren't you nervous being out here alone? It seems to me people aren't as afraid as they should be. Would you believe girls are still hitchhiking?"

"Yes. No, I mean, I wouldn't believe it. But it did occur to me that he might be hanging around. I was careful."

She felt reprimanded, like a small child, and hoped the light was too poor for him to see her discomfort.

"Mr. D'Amico, I wanted to tell you, I hope you didn't mind the way they were talking. It's just hysterical. I think people really know you can't pull a murderer out of a hat. You're doing a great job, and it isn't easy, especially when you don't even know where to begin."

She had babbled too much, in her uncertainty as to whether she was saying it right. She wanted to say more, to keep him with her, and ask his help. But she did not know quite how, or for what.

Instead she held out her hand. He took it, gave it a squeeze, and did not immediately let go. The moment seemed to stretch. All the while she felt something almost ready to put itself into words, but finally it eluded her. It must have been the intensity of her in those moments that made him hold tightly to her hand.

"Are you here alone?" he asked as he released her.

"No, I came with friends. It was so stuffy in there, I felt faint."

"I was going to warn you, always check your car before you get in alone, especially at night."

"I don't have my car here, but thanks."

"In that case, maybe I'd better give you a lift home."

"Oh, it's way out of your way. And my friends will be looking for me."

"Then I'd suggest you go back inside. They're going to be in there a while. They're talking about forming some civilian patrol groups."

She saw a few other people leaving, but not the Farands. They would be in the thick of it. They must have helped to organize the meeting itself.

"I don't particularly want to go back," she said. "I just didn't like the atmosphere. It got so ugly. And stuffy."

He threw back his head, but the laugh that emerged was only a low chuckle.

"Don't mind them," he said. "People get that way. A lot

of the shouting is pure egotism. I'm going for a bite to eat. Haven't eaten all day, and the civilian patrol stuff is none of my business. Do you want a lift? I could take you home first, or you can come and have a hamburger with me on the way."

She hesitated, wanting to get back to her children. But this might be the quickest way yet, and she did want to talk to him, if only to find out what he knew.

She left a note on the Farands' windshield and drove with D'Amico to the lower part of the village near the railroad tracks. He found Ralph's Pizzeria still open and ordered a whole large pie with sausages and mushrooms, and coffee for both of them.

"If you haven't eaten all day," she pointed out, "this isn't really going to give you your basic nutrients."

"No, but it keeps me going. On a job like this, when you gotta keep working twenty-four hours, you substitute food for sleep. And if you don't get a chance to eat, either, you find yourself blacking out."

"Good heavens, I hope those people back there at the meeting appreciate what you're doing for them. But doesn't your wife mind you inviting strange women for dinner, instead of going home?"

"She might if I had a wife," he answered without looking at her. "I'd level with her. But I haven't had a wife in fifteen years."

"Oh."

"That's why it's good to have company sometimes. What about your husband? I guess he wouldn't make a big deal over this, would he? Or you wouldn't have come."

"He isn't going to know," she said. "I really don't know whether he'd make a big deal. He's—kind of odd sometimes."

"Odd? In what way?"

She could hardly tell him about her sex life. "Oh, I don't know. He just— Well, he's moody. Sometimes he seems very distant."

"Yeah?"

She really had no right to be discussing Carl with this man. "I'm sorry. I don't know what got into me, talking like that."

He was silent, absently spinning the pepper shaker with his fingers.

"Your husband's staying with the kids tonight?" he finally asked. "How many kids do you have?"

"Three at the moment." She explained about Adam and Gail, and Mary Ellen visiting. "So we have his, hers, and ours. We were both married before. He was divorced and I was widowed."

"You, too?"

"My husband was killed by a mugger two years ago."

"Rough." He twirled the pepper shaker again. "You're probably up to here with murder. So am I. That must be hard on your kid, too. She'd be old enough to remember. Does she know what happened?"

"Yes, but not all the details. Of course she asked what happened to him, and I had to tell her."

"How old was she then? About seven, right?" His computerlike mind amazed her. How could he remember Gail so well? "That's just the age when they're beginning to understand that death is forever."

"Do you have children?"

"No," he said. "Didn't have time. We were only married a few months."

"And?" she asked softly.

He shrugged. "Cancer."

"She must have been very young."

"Just twenty."

"That's terrible."

"Yeah, it was. But no worse than what's going on now. And maybe even a little easier to accept. At least it's an act of God, even if you can't help wondering why God would do a thing like that."

He really must have wondered, she thought. He must have been very bitter, never to have married again.

"So it's over and done with," he said as their pizza arrived, "for you and me both. You were lucky to find another good man."

She was silent, and discovered she was not particularly hungry as she delicately nibbled on a crust.

"What do you think of that civilian patrol idea?" she asked, scooping up a dripping rope of mozzarella cheese. "Is it a good thing, or do they just get in the way?"

"I don't know, in a place like this. In a basically rural situation, it's hard for the police to cover the whole area. You don't know when or where he's going to strike. The best part about it, though, is citizen involvement. You've got them watching, you've got them alert, the girls will be more careful, we hope, and we might even come up with a lead this way. It could act as some kind of deterrent, too."

"Did you find where the murders took place?" she asked. "Carl, my husband, said that's what you were looking for."

"The first two. We had the place under surveillance, and then the third one happened."

"In a different place?"

"Yup."

"Where— You aren't going to tell me, are you? Was it near there? In the woods? It can't have been Mr. Lattimer. You'd have arrested him by now."

His face was unreadable as he reached for another slice of pizza.

"You don't arrest somebody," he said, "just because a murder took place on his property."

"It did?"

"We found pieces of clothing, and we found a place where the body might have been kept before it was put out there in the woods."

"Why are you telling me this?"

"Doesn't matter now. We thought we could get him to come back there, but somehow he must have known. That's why we kept it from the press."

"Where is the place?"

"You know the Lattimer property? He's got a lot of little outbuildings. There's a sort of stone shed where the brook comes up. It's built around the spring, very cool inside. They must have used it for refrigeration."

They. The Lattimers. For one exultant moment she thought they had found the killer. But they couldn't have. Another murder had happened under their noses.

"Are you watching anybody in particular?" she asked.

"Anybody and everybody. Now I told you this as a friend," he added, "because, like I say, it doesn't matter anymore about the killer, he knew we'd stumbled on the place. But I'd appreciate not having the general public all over."

"I won't say a word." She was still amazed that he had mentioned it to her at all.

"Mr. D'Amico—"

"Frank," he said. "If we're eating together, we should skip the formalities. Unless you don't want to."

"You're right. I'm Joyce."

"I have a cousin named Joyce."

"Really?"

"No, come to think of it, it's Joy. I've got about fifty cousins. Hard to keep track."

"Frank—what sort of person do you think it is?"

He set down his coffee cup. "You heard what the shrink said. That's all I can tell you."

"I want to know what you think. I want to know how there can be a person like that, with the people around him, his family, if he has one, the people who see him every day, not realizing it. Wouldn't there be something about him? Wouldn't he— Do you think they're protecting him, maybe? His family? And what about the blood? Wouldn't he get blood on himself sometimes?"

Frank picked up the coffee cup again, drank from it, stared at it for a moment, then set it down.

"There could be a lot of things," he said. "There are a lot of people walking around who are kind of flaky. Would you necessarily think they're homicidal? Especially if it's someone you know well, you probably wouldn't think so. There was a woman who worked right next to Son of Sam at the post office, talked to him every day, even talked about the murders, and never guessed he was the guy."

She nodded. He took another slice of pizza, chewed a bite and swallowed it.

"Then a lot of times," he went on, "these people disassociate themselves. They commit a homicide, and afterward they honestly have this feeling that it was somebody else that did it. There was a guy in Chicago back in the forties. He blamed it all on a person named George. He really believed George existed, even had letters from him, but in fact, George was only a part of himself."

"How weird."

"Sometimes they try that sort of thing to cop an insanity plea, but usually these random killers are bananas to begin with, or they wouldn't be doing what they do. Right?"

"Do you think he wrote that letter to the newspaper?"

"I think so. I think it was probably genuine. I think he was trying to copy Jack the Ripper. He wrote letters, you know."

"It sounded like somebody who's not too well educated."

"Joyce, anybody who's educated can write like someone who's not. It's the other way around they can't do it."

"Then you think he—he disguised himself—that way?"

"That's what I think. What's the matter?"

"I don't know. It just bothers me. I don't know why."

"You think an educated person wouldn't commit that sort of murder?"

"No, I don't mean that. Educated people can be crazy, too. It's just— I don't know."

She picked up a piece of mushroom that had been left on the plate. It was cold. She dropped it.

"What about the blood?" she asked. "How can he do it without getting blood on himself, and why doesn't somebody see it?"

"Who knows? But look, he kills by strangulation, right? After the body's dead, there's no pulse, so the blood doesn't spurt like it does from a living artery. Hey, am I making you sick?"

She sighed. "No, I just wasn't all that hungry to begin with." She saw the newspaper pictures in a row, the three smiling faces, then saw them contort as their necks were squeezed, saw the corpses sliced open.

"Look, Joyce, I'm sorry." Unconsciously, it seemed, his hand reached out and closed over hers. "You probably think I get used to these things. I never do. It's always a human being. But this is my daily work. I get so I can talk about it, but it's not very nice at the dinner table, is it? And I sort of forgot you weren't a colleague."

"I suppose that's a tribute." She smiled weakly.

"Right, it is. But after what you went through with your first husband killed, I sure wish you didn't have to have this now."

He took his hand away from hers, and as much as a solid man like D'Amico could, seemed flustered to have found it there.

He demolished the last of the pizza, then drove her home, insisting it was not out of the way at all.

"Thanks for coming with me," he said as she left the car. "I enjoyed your company." In the dark, she thought his eyes searched her face.

"I enjoyed it, too," she said. "And I hope you get that break real soon."

She turned to go into the house, and saw Carl in the darkened kitchen doorway.

"Who was that?" Carl asked. "That wasn't the Farands' car."

"Oh . . . no . . . I left early. It got so hot in there I couldn't breathe, and the Farands were staying forever. Somebody else gave me a ride."

"Who?"

"Oh—a policeman."

Carl's mouth opened to ask another question, but no sound came out. What he wanted was an explanation, she was sure. Why couldn't he ask?

"He was coming up here anyway," she said, and brilliantly added, "I guess they're keeping an eye on Mr. Lattimer. And naturally they're terrified when they see a woman going around by herself. They don't want any more bodies."

As she spoke, her mind was far away, for it had suddenly occurred to her that Mr. Lattimer could not possibly be the killer. None of the murdered girls had lived around there, none would have had any reason to be there, especially Toni Lemich, coming home from work on the train and living not far from the station.

The killer would have had to have a car.

The police, of course, already knew that, and therefore all their talk about forcing girls into a car at gunpoint.

She slipped off her shoes and started toward the stairs, giving wide berth to the naked, black picture window, which seemed to be an eye staring in from outside.

Carl followed her. "So you just got into a car with a strange man—"

"He's hardly a strange man," she replied. "You met him

yourself, he's the chief of police. He was only doing his job of protecting the women in this town. Otherwise you might have a murdered wife by now."

She did not like this jealousy. She did not like anything about him at the moment that seemed exaggerated or abnormal.

She even began to wonder if she still loved him. But her mind balked at that question. She was not ready to face it—or anything else.

16

They went swimming again the next Wednesday afternoon. When they came home, Mary Ellen took a shower to wash off the lake water. They could hear her singing to herself. Gail was playing on the floor of the master bedroom, near Adam's crib, setting up a paper doll family.

"Mommy, the telephone's ringing."

Joyce had not heard it. She slid onto her bed to pick it up from the night table.

"That you, Joyce?"

It was what her mother always said. Joyce's heart gave an anxious bump. "Mom! Where are you calling from?"

"Home." A long distance call in the middle of the day. "Honey, Dad's gone to the hospital. It's his kidneys again. He just collapsed this morning and they had to operate."

"Is it bad?"

"Can't tell yet. That's why I'm calling. They had to do an emergency operation. . . . Hello?"

Joyce was busy making plans. Could she take the children with her? Was Adam old enough to travel? And what would she do with Mary Ellen?

"I'm coming," she said. "I—guess I'll fly." It was expensive, but she could not see Adam on a train for all those hours. "Maybe tomorrow, if I can get reservations. Is that okay?"

As far as her mother knew, it would be. Dad had at least pulled through the operation. Her brother Pat would meet her at the airport.

She hung up the phone, feeling sad and empty. It wasn't time yet for this kind of thing. Her parents, although she rarely saw them, were fixtures in her life. She expected them to live forever.

She called the airline, sure that they would be unable to

110

give her reservations, but it was the middle of the week and they had seats.

At five-thirty she began calling Barbara. She knew Barbara worked in the office of a department store not far from her home. She was unclear whether department store offices kept office hours or department store hours. In any case, Barbara was not yet home.

She tried again every fifteen minutes, and finally asked Mary Ellen when her mother usually got home from work.

"About a quarter to six," Mary Ellen answered dreamily, "but I don't think she's there right now."

"I know she's not there. I—"

"I mean I think she's away on vacation. She was going away for a while."

"Alone? She'd take a vacation alone?" Meaning without Mary Ellen.

"She's not alone."

"Oh."

Mary Ellen did not know where she had gone. Nantucket, or Atlantic City. She did not even seem to know her mother's tastes. Joyce asked, "Is there anybody near where you live—?"

Mary Ellen shook her head. "Everybody's away. All my friends."

"And you couldn't stay here, you'd be alone all day."

A violent shake of the head. "I don't want to stay with Daddy. Please, Joyce?"

Joyce hadn't time to think about it now, but the vehemence disturbed her. She suggested Olivia. Mary Ellen rejected that, too. "She'll make me come back to Daddy. He'll say he wants me, and she does everything he wants. Please, Joyce, couldn't I go with you? I'll help. I'll take care of Adam for you."

Joyce was touched. The child sounded desperate. But, really, it was all they needed, in a house crowded with her brothers and sisters and their families, a house where death hovered. If Mary Ellen were really a part of her new family, it would have been different, but she was only a visitor who could not share their emotions about Dad.

Still, what else? It was getting later by the minute. The plane would be filled, whatever they decided. Mary Ellen stood waiting, her face drawn and her fingers clenched. Joyce gave her a tired smile.

"Okay, I just hope it won't be too dreary for you. And maybe it would be a good idea after all to have you along to help with Adam. I'll be spending a lot of time at the hospital."

To her surprise, Mary Ellen gave her arm a little squeeze before she scurried away. Perceptive child, she knew she was intruding. Probably, Joyce thought in a burst of generosity, she didn't even want to, but what was the answer?

She was able to get another seat on the plane, and it didn't matter if they couldn't all sit together. Then she called her mother to tell her what flight they would be on and to explain about Mary Ellen. Just as she was hanging up the phone, Carl came home.

She watched his face slowly draw together while she told him of her plans. Had he expected to be consulted?

He burst out, "Why do you have to go? There's nothing you can do for him."

She could scarcely believe it. "Carl, people just *go* when their parents are sick. He may even be dying. How could I not go? I love my father, understand?"

"What about me?"

"I—love you, too."

That, apparently, was not what he meant. "I need you here."

"Oh, come on, you managed by yourself for years. Don't be a baby. I should think you'd be glad to get us all out and have some peace and quiet for a few days."

"All of you? Where's Mary Ellen going?"

She told him about Mary Ellen, with Barbara being on vacation.

His face tightened again, but it looked different this time. Not angry. It was something else.

"Why can't you leave her here?" he asked almost eagerly. "She'll be all right."

"How can I, with you away all day? Especially now, with the murders."

"There's a weekend coming up, remember?"

"What about after the weekend?"

"How the hell long are you staying?"

"A week, maybe. I don't know. I just don't know how things are with my father."

"Stay as long as you want," he said, his voice now soft and reasonable, "and leave Mary Ellen here. She'll be all right. Don't forget, she's my kid. I have something to say about it."

Cancel the reservation? No, she couldn't. He had something to say, but he wasn't thinking. All day tomorrow, and next week, too, at least some of it.

And Mary Ellen had been so definite. Not about staying alone, but being with him.

He did not seem aware that she had already made Mary Ellen's reservation. During dinner he all but ignored Joyce, and talked to Mary Ellen about the weekend they would spend together. The child answered in monosyllables, scarcely daring to look at him.

I've got to tell him, Joyce thought.

But she was afraid to.

Did he really think it was feasible for Mary Ellen to stay? Of course he wanted companionship. He had sounded so very eager to be alone with her. Barbara had never let her stay with him before he married Joyce. They were only allowed to visit with each other during the day.

Crazy Barbara. Bitter. Spiteful.

But Mary Ellen did not want to be alone with him, either.

Could she ask Mary Ellen point-blank what the problem was? Why she didn't want to stay?

No, she couldn't.

And anyway, it was nothing. Only his strictness. All that nagging about clothes. Nag, nag, nag.

Probably he thought he was being a parent. Felt awkward with her. A father and daughter, awkward with each other. She was growing up.

Yes, growing up . . .

Joyce stopped thinking about it then. She had reached a dead end, a sort of black curtain. Something she couldn't see, but which barred her way.

She spent the rest of the evening packing. It took a long time, with so many things to remember for the baby.

Carl came upstairs as she was finishing. He leaned

against the dresser, an after-dinner glass of whiskey in his hand, and watched her, saying nothing.

Finally she broke the silence, with trivia, anything.

"I wish I could leave you a full refrigerator. I just didn't have a chance to shop after I heard. But you can pick up something on Saturday."

He did not reply. She wondered aloud about long-term parking at La Guardia Airport.

"Long term?" he asked hoarsely.

"Well, you know, for a few days. Otherwise you're paying by the hour, which is ridiculous. Or maybe I shouldn't drive. The travel agency on Grand Street runs an airport taxi, but I don't know if it stops at La Guardia."

She watched him take a long drink from his glass.

"I wish we didn't have to go," she said. "Not like this. I wish it could be a fun trip, with you, too. But when Mom called me like that, she sounded as if he might be dying, or at least she wasn't sure. I can't *not* go."

He turned and, without a word, left the room. She hated for it to be like that, but felt almost relieved to see him go. After that he stayed downstairs, poring over the newspaper, watching the television news. He said no more about Mary Ellen.

Bone-tired, she crawled into bed at last, and was not even aware when he got in beside her. And thirty miles away, as New York City turned off its lights and prepared to sleep, a man staggered into the headquarters of the Twentieth Precinct on West Eighty-second Street and announced that he was turning himself in.

"I killed some girls out in the country there." He jerked his thumb toward the east, which was Long Island. "I killed 'em. I cut 'em up and took off their clothes. They're looking for me there."

"Where was this at?" the sergeant at the desk inquired. The man smelled. He smelled of phoniness, sweat, and booze. He wore a white tee shirt and stained gray pants, and a stubble hid his receding chin.

"Out there in Westchester," the man explained. "In Cedarville."

At least he had the right community. "Do you live in Cedarville?"

"No, but I go out there. I got friends there."

Further investigation produced the fact that the man had once lived in the vicinity of Cedarville, and his old mother had recently died in a nursing home there. Enough to unhinge the mind of a loony, perhaps, but despite the probable falseness of his confession, arrangements were made for him to be transported to Cedarville for questioning.

The ever-hungry media pounced on the story, although no information was officially released. By three o'clock, news of the man's surrender flashed over the air waves and was picked up by a small portable radio resting on a bed in Cedarville.

Joyce sat up, her earplug falling to the pillow. Quickly she retrieved it and poked it back into her ear.

"Carl! Carl, it's over! A man gave himself up!"

The massive shoulder lowered to the bed. He lay on his back, his eyes half open, little slits in the dim gray light.

"Huh?" he grunted.

"The murderer just gave himself up! We're free!"

"How the hell do you know?" His voice sounded slurred, as though he had been drinking, but it was only sleep.

"The radio. I just heard it on the radio."

"What the hell . . . radio . . ." He turned his head and looked at the glowing face of the clock radio.

"Your little portable. I was trying to get a weather report for tomorrow, and I used an earplug so it wouldn't bother you. Don't you understand? It's over now! The man gave himself up."

"Aw, just some fag." He settled down as before, on his side.

"What do you mean?"

"Just some jerk. Wants attention."

He was wrong. It wouldn't have gotten as far as the radio if it were only some jerk wanting attention.

She listened a while longer, but there was no more news about the man on Eighty-second Street.

Then she lay and stared at the ceiling through darkness that looked like black fuzz, and thought about the man. She rejected something deep inside that told her Carl was probably right.

It had to be that man.

17

She felt relieved that Carl had no intention of driving them to the airport and seeing them off. It would have been sticky about Mary Ellen, although he had not mentioned Mary Ellen since dinnertime. She did not know whether he finally realized she was going and was resigned to it, or whether he still expected to find her in the house when he came home from work that night.

Rather than cope with public transportation, she had decided to take her own car to the airport. There was a rush of last-minute packing, and the clearing up of breakfast, and they were off.

"You understand, Mary Ellen," she told the girl as they drove, "this is not exactly a pleasure trip. You and Gail will have fun, but the rest of us are going to be a little sad, and we'll have a lot to do."

"I know," Mary Ellen replied. "I told you, I'm going to take care of Adam."

She understood. But did Gail? Gail had seen so much death already in her nine years.

Joyce had intended to call Carl from the airport, but the plane was already boarding when they checked in. Perhaps it was just as well. He might have found out about Mary Ellen. She did not know why that bothered her so much, or why she couldn't have reasoned with him.

Once they boarded the plane, she felt safe. He couldn't get her now. She wondered why she was thinking that way.

It was because she was afraid of his anger. Nothing more. She had listened to the radio again that morning. The man was being taken to Cedarville for questioning. By the time she came back, everything would be under control. Gail could play outside again and Mary Ellen could ride on David's motorcycle.

And Carl might have forgiven her for taking away his daughter.

The plane began to move, taxiing toward the runway. She stared out at the speeding earth and wished she had gone to visit her family more often. All her childhood seemed suddenly clearer, and she mourned the things that were past. They were more precious than she had realized eleven years ago when she could hardly wait to get away and see the world.

She hadn't seen the world exactly, but had had her fill of instability in those years with Larry and the struggling theater crowd. A lot of it had been fun, but afterward she was ready to settle down.

And she had, with a good man. Frank D'Amico had called him that, but Frank didn't know everything. He didn't know, for instance, about the blowups with Mary Ellen, and the moodiness, and that night when he had cursed her in bed, but not her, it was someone else. She had thought she knew Carl. Now it was as though a wall shut him away from her. He was different, changed. She did not know him at all. She was not even sure she wanted to go back to him.

But that was over now. The man had confessed. Maybe it would be like before.

Perhaps it was her own terrors that made him seem different.

The flight was short, and the Pittsburgh terminal unfamiliar. She had never flown here before, but always come by train because it was cheaper. And she hadn't even done that very often.

She stood surrounded by their luggage, holding Adam in a shoulder sling, and waiting to be found.

Gail hopped like a pogo stick. "There's Uncle Pat." She had recognized him before Joyce did. He had cut his hair and grown a mustache.

His eyes widened when he saw that Joyce's party included Mary Ellen. Mom must have forgotten to tell him. He had brought his own family to the airport, his wife Meredith, three-year-old John, and the new baby that was born a month before Adam. Probably he wondered how

they would all fit into his car. Joyce hurried to introduce
Mary Ellen and explain why she was there.

Mary Ellen bit her lip. "I guess I'm going to be in the
way, aren't I?"

"Not at all," said Meredith. "It's a big house, with loads
of room inside and out."

Mary Ellen smiled thinly. She had not been talking
about space. Probably, until she met these people, Joyce's
family had been vague and unreal to her.

As it turned out, space was no problem in the car, either, for Pat had a van. It was a forty-mile drive to Cork.
Joyce sat in the front beside Pat and was brought up to
date on family affairs, including their father's health.

"They don't know how it's going to turn out," Pat said.
"He got through the operation okay, but you can't tell.
How's Carl?"

He had never met Carl. None of the family had. Joyce
had not been back to Cork since the summer Larry died,
when she and Gail tried to console themselves with a two-
week visit.

"Oh, he's all right. He'll be taking his vacation week after next." As though to apologize for Carl's not being with
her.

"When are you going to bring him down here?"

"Well, actually . . ." How to explain about Carl? He
was not the least bit interested in meeting her family.
"Why don't you come and visit us sometime?"

"Maybe, when the kids are older. I hear you've been
having a wild summer up in Cedarville."

"How did you hear that?" She had not written to them
about the murders.

"Newspaper," he said.

"It's been in the papers here?"

"It's news, isn't it?"

She supposed it was. Three brutal sex murders in one
small community. A community that thought it was safe.

"It's over now," she was glad to tell him. "A man
confessed."

"Yeah? When?"

"Last night. A man in New York City. Imagine."

"That's a big relief," said Pat.

"It sure is."

She watched out of the window as the territory grew more familiar, changing from Pittsburgh to its suburbs, and then to the country. Finally they were in the outskirts of Cork, if it could be called an outskirt when Cork itself was so small.

Mary Ellen crept up behind her to look over her shoulder. "I never was in Pennsylvania before."

Pat asked, "Did you expect it to be a different color, like on the map?"

They passed the new shopping center and then entered Main Street, where the older stores were, the stores Joyce remembered from her childhood. She pointed out the highlights to Gail and Mary Ellen. Up that street was the high school, you couldn't see it from here. And there was the Tower of Pizza, always mobbed with kids who scorned the school cafeteria and brown bag lunches.

It made her think of that supper with Frank D'Amico, and the feel of his hand of hers.

And there, she told Mary Ellen, was the five-and-ten-cent store where she used to browse endlessly through the cosmetics, thinking that, if only she could find the right eyeshadow, glamour and a thrilling life were just around the corner.

Mary Ellen exclaimed, "I love this place. I like it better than White Plains, it's so cute and cozy. You must have had fun when you were a kid."

"I really couldn't wait to grow up," Joyce answered with a rueful laugh. "I thought that was when the fun would begin."

Then they were out of town again, on a blacktop road with trees and fields on either side. And then turning into the driveway. She knew every tuft of grass growing among its pebbles.

And the house. It was home, and yet no longer home. She was surprised at how shabby it looked, and embarrassed that Mary Ellen should see it that way. It hadn't been painted in years.

Her mother did not come out to the porch to meet them. Probably she was at the hospital, Pat said as he opened the unlocked front door. Joyce had forgotten that they left the door unlocked.

"I wish she wouldn't do that. Times have changed, Pat, I should know, and now she's here alone."

"You can tell her," he replied, "and it won't make any impression. She's always done it."

They left the children at the house with Meredith, and Pat drove Joyce to the hospital. Her mother was in a chair by the bedside, knitting. With a little cry of pleasure, she stuffed her knitting into its bag and rose to embrace them.

Their father lay half sleeping, his face a pale yellow-white, a plastic tube for oxygen in his nose and another for intravenous feeding in his arm.

Do we all have to end like this? Joyce wondered as she bent to kiss his cheek. And then she thought: How much better this way, cared for and comforted, than like those girls.

He greeted her weakly and his hand trembled as she held it. She chattered to him about the children, about the baby, whom he had not seen, and could not until "next time," as she put it, and about how she had had to bring Mary Ellen. He watched her for a while, and then his eyes closed and his hand relaxed.

"I guess I wore him out," she whispered to her mother, who stood up and beckoned her into the hall.

"It's just the operation," her mother explained. "He'll get better, they promised me, and I told them to be honest. I didn't know that when I called you. It's good that you came. I hope he doesn't think—"

"I tried to make it sound as if we're just on a little vacation," Joyce said. "And I'm glad we came, too. It's nice to see everybody."

The next days were crowded with relatives, at both the hospital and the house. She was ashamed that she had neglected them for two whole years, and for a long time before that. Mary Ellen was shocked to learn that no one in the family had seen Adam, and he was now almost two months old.

"That happens all the time," Joyce explained. "People move away from home, and—"

"It's not going to happen to me," Mary Ellen insisted. "I like your big family. I wish I had a big family."

"You have Adam, and probably there will be more.

And maybe your mother will marry again and you'll have full-time brothers and sisters."

"She won't. She likes it this way. And even if she did, I'd be too old for them."

"Too old" was an odd phrase, coming from a twelve-year-old, but spoken with such an air of resignation that it was not funny.

Mary Ellen added, "They could have had more babies after me. It'd be more fun for me now. They didn't get divorced till I was four years old. There was plenty of time."

Plenty of time, yes. Joyce groped to remember something Barbara had said. Some question that, at the time, had seemed impertinent, but now she wondered. Had it been the same with Barbara?

She wished she could recall the question, or statement, or whatever it was. She wished she could talk to Barbara now. There had been so many innuendoes, half spoken, half asked. She had turned them all aside, but now she needed to know. There *was* something wrong.

But it didn't matter so much anymore. The man had turned himself in. It was only between Carl and herself, and there was no hurry about that.

Every day she visited the hospital, leaving her children in the care of a brother or sister, all of whom lived nearby. Once she left Mary Ellen in charge. She worried that Gail might be nervous, thinking of the murders, but Gail had not brought them with her. She blossomed in Pennsylvania.

"Why can't we live here, Mommy?" she asked when they took a walk to the stream in back of the house. "It's so nice. Why couldn't we stay here when we came after Daddy died?"

"You didn't want to then, remember?" said Joyce. "You wanted to get back to the city and your friends."

Or maybe only to everything that was familiar. And so had Joyce. They had never considered staying.

She put a hand on Gail's shoulder. "If we lived here, when you got to be a teenager, you'd find it deadly. I did. I took off for New York exactly one week after graduation."

And never came back. And was glad.

But when she thought about going back now, something

cold filled her stomach. Even though the man had given himself up and the murders were all over, there was that lump of dread. She could not seem to make it go away.

Perhaps because, although she tried very hard, she did not quite believe the man's confession.

18

She had not talked to Carl since leaving home, not even to call and tell him they had arrived safely. She was afraid because of her deception about Mary Ellen. Still, she knew she would have to face him someday, and it was better to pave the way over the telephone. She dialed the number on Monday night at seven o'clock. He should have been home, but perhaps the train was late.

She tried again at nine and then at ten. The cold, hard lump began to climb into her throat. He always came home—except on that other Monday night, but that was because of work at the office.

She gave up trying then. If he was going to be out all night, she didn't want to know it. She found herself feeling shaky as she undressed and went to bed. She tried to believe that everything was all right. Over and over again she said it, but could not get rid of the lump.

She had made return reservations for Thursday morning. Her father was out of danger and her mother beginning to show signs of strain. She knew it was time to take the children and ship out. On Tuesday she confirmed the reservations, and then in the evening, tried again to reach Carl.

This time he answered.

She expected an explosion, because of Mary Ellen. Instead he remarked calmly, "So you finally decided to come back," and it was she who exploded.

"What do you mean 'finally'? It's only been since Thursday. Wouldn't you give your mother that much time if she were sick?"

She knew he would. That, and a whole lot more.

"Anyway," she added, "I thought you'd be glad we're coming."

123

"I am. Very glad. It's been too quiet around here."

"I don't know if I appreciate that."

"I mean without the kids. They're part of you, aren't they?"

She supposed they were, but it made her feel like an earth mother.

"What exactly do you mean by quiet? I hope you mean nothing's been happening."

"Oh, a few things, I guess. The alarm goes off in the morning—that's a happening, isn't it?—I shave, cook my breakfast, catch the train . . ."

"How perfectly idyllic. What did you do last night? I tried to call you."

"Last night? Let's see. I went to the movies. Came home late."

"The movies?"

They laughed about it together as he described his trip to the movies. He sounded normal, natural, playful. Her misgivings thawed.

"At least you've been surviving," she said. "And good old Cedarville, too. What happened with that man they arrested?"

"What man?"

"The one who turned himself in just before I left. Remember, on the radio?"

"Oh, that. I told you he wasn't anything. They had to let him go. I told you."

"They let him go?"

"Sure. I told you he was just some jerk."

"Oh . . . well . . ." Her hand had become weak again, her fingers almost releasing the telephone.

"I hope they know what they're doing," she said.

Frank D'Amico must have known. He would not have done it without a good reason. The man was not the right one, that was the reason.

"Okay," Carl prompted at her continued and busy silence, "I'll see you Thursday, then. What time are you coming? Do you need any help getting from the airport?"

"No, I took the car, as you probably noticed. I'll be all right. And I do thank you for letting me borrow Mary Ellen. She's been very helpful."

"Glad to hear it." And that was that.

She set the telephone back in its place.

No, please, you shouldn't have let him go.

But why not, if he wasn't the right man? Did crazy killers ever really give themselves up? Or did they have to be hunted down? She tried to think of a case. It was the sane murderer who gave himself up. Killed his wife in the heat of anger and then, weeping, called the police.

If that man was not the murderer, who was?

She remembered how she had wondered, after the near-drowning incident, about Anita's own family. But Foster had carried himself so well at the town meeting, with that marvelous speech.

Bruce Cheskill, who had made a pass at a baby-sitter . . .

Or anybody. It could have been anybody. And she was going back, and taking her girls back, to where the killer still roamed at large.

19

They flew to New York at noon on Thursday. The air felt familiar, smoggy and gritty, as they left the terminal and walked toward their car. She should have been glad to come home, but she was not. Something hung over her, something deathly and terrible.

He had sounded so cheerful on the phone, telling about the movie. Why, then, did she feel this way?

They drove over the Triborough Bridge and up the Major Deegan Expressway through the hectic Bronx. As soon as they reached the green of Van Cortlandt Park, she felt they were almost home. There was still Yonkers, but that was Westchester already, and after Yonkers they were really out in the country.

They left the Expressway at Elmsford and followed local roads to Cedarville. Entering the town, she found it as quiet as Carl had said it was. Four little girls played hopscotch on the sidewalk under the watchful eye of an old woman rocking on a front porch. A press car was parked in front of the police station—they were not going to give up these murders easily—and Mr. Lattimer came out of the liquor store with a brown shopping bag to begin his long journey up the hill to his home.

"Don't give him a lift," said Gail. "He'll smell up the car."

"I doubt if we'd have room anyway," Joyce replied, unwilling to admit her own prejudice. Dirty clothes she might have tolerated, but not the smell. She could not help a pang of guilt as they passed him, but hardened herself. Despite the improbability, he still might have been the killer.

Certainly he had the best opportunity, living alone as he did, and with all those outbuildings, which Frank said had been used in the killings. And the best motive, too: an unbalanced mind.

Again she felt guilty, for she was not really sure how unbalanced his mind was. He lived alone because he had no one to live with. He lived in poverty because he was poor. And he kept to himself—because he was a pariah? Or was he a pariah because he kept to himself?

She turned in at their driveway, and the house came into view. It looked strange and unwelcoming with the doors and windows closed. For a dizzy moment she thought Carl had gone away and left them, but of course he had only gone to work.

She wished he could have been there, or someone could have been, to spare her that slight shudder of dread on unlocking the door into a house that was empty.

As soon as she was inside, the dread went away. She was home. It was exactly as she had left it, almost timeless, and waiting for her. If anything, it was neater. Not a crumb on the kitchen table. Every dish in the cupboard. That was Carl's way.

"Shall I put Adam to bed?" Mary Ellen asked.

"For now," said Joyce. "I'll have to feed him soon, but I think I'll call your father first and tell him we're home."

She took off her shoes, her pantyhose and traveling clothes, and put on a pink seersucker shift with large strawberry pockets. As she sat at the kitchen table, she found herself watching the screen door. You never could tell. After all, the man who confessed was at large again. She got up, locked the screen, and then dialed Carl's office.

"Hi," she said when he came on the phone. "Just thought I'd let you know we're back."

"Are you calling from home?" he asked.

"Where else from?"

"I thought you might be at the airport."

"No, we made straight for the car. And I want to congratulate you on keeping this place so neat and tidy."

He said, "Did you see the newspapers I left for you?"

"No."

"On the coffee table. I thought you might want me to save them, since you're so interested, even going to that meeting and all." He chuckled softly. "Don't throw them out when you're finished."

"Read—about it?"

"The latest. Our little hamlet's claim to fame. I have another call waiting. See you tonight."

Upstairs in his crib, Adam began to cry. It was not until later that she found time to look at the papers.

They were piled neatly on the coffee table, every edge lined up, and carefully arranged in chronological order. On the bottom was Thursday, the day she had left. On the top, Wednesday, with the big fat Sunday edition near the middle.

She lifted off the top *Times* and discovered the *Daily News* underneath. The very front page. Giant pictures. Again that slow, thudding pound of her heart.

She did not want to know when it happened. She put her hand over the caption and read only far enough to learn that it was another young girl, a thirteen-year-old. Probably hitchhiking, the paper said.

She could not avoid the date. She knew it anyway, it was yesterday's paper, so it could not have been last night, or even the night before, since this was a morning paper. If Sunday, it would have been an aftermath, not splashed all over page one. Monday night, while she had been snug in her childhood home, and he, a lonely bachelor at the movies, with the telephone ringing and ringing in an empty house.

At the movies. He had laughed about it. Hadn't been to the flicks in years. Kind of funny to walk into a theater. The five dollars wasn't so funny, though. He had refrained from buying popcorn, but they still sold it, just like when he was a kid.

Ringing and ringing in an empty house, while he had gone to the movies. Alone. Why couldn't he have come home and watched television? Was the house too quiet?

She let the paper fall into her lap. She couldn't read any more. As she folded it, Mary Ellen came in from the garden with grass stains on her bare knees.

"Well, what's been going on?" Mary Ellen asked, seeing the newspapers.

"Do you really want to know?" said Joyce.

"You mean there was another?"

"Not, thank God, in the woods, but that doesn't make any difference. The poor girl. It doesn't matter where she was found."

"Where was she found?" Mary Ellen could take it.

"In some bushes along the road between here and Ossining. Thirteen years old."

Mary Ellen whistled sympathetically. Joyce went on, "It says she was probably hitchhiking. I hope you know better than to hitchhike."

Mary Ellen sat down on the sofa and picked up the paper Joyce had folded. She noticed her knees and tried to brush off the stain. "I've been weeding your flowers, Joyce. Hope you don't mind."

"I'm delighted."

"It's fun, having flowers. I wish we could have flowers. Maybe I'll get some houseplants." Mary Ellen buried herself in the newspaper.

Why hadn't he told her?

He had let her come home thinking all was peaceful, and then made her find out like this. It was almost coy, the way he had directed her to that pile of papers.

Perhaps he hadn't wanted her to worry. Perhaps it had slipped his mind.

It couldn't have. He had saved all the papers. He must have been thinking of it always.

What if he had gone to the movies, not on Monday night as he said, but Friday or Saturday? He could still chuckle about the price and the popcorn, and she would never know.

She wandered outside and stood in the shade of an oak tree, staring at the flower border for a minute or two before she actually saw it. The flowers did look neater. Poor Mary Ellen, wanting a piece of earth she could call her own.

But perhaps Mary Ellen was actually safer in her city apartment. Joyce looked up at the tall oak tree, at the other trees, a gently rustling canopy over the soft lawn. It had seemed pure enchantment when they bought the house, clean and perfect for Gail and the children to come. Now it was secret, and too alone. Safety was that gritty sidewalk where everyone played together, and the building superintendents, forever tinkering with their cars,

were always there, like guardians, alert for anything unusual. They knew everybody on the block.

But she loved it here. She loved the greenness and the
waving canopy. And she loved—

She did not love Carl any longer. There was too much
strangeness, too many doubts.

She remembered the night he had called her a whore.
But he was speaking to someone else. Someone who, all
unknowing, had hurt him once, and he—

No, she was being ridiculous. If Carl knew what she
was thinking— No, no, no.

She returned to the house. Mary Ellen had gone upstairs. She rearranged the papers, not as neatly as Carl
would have liked, and went into the kitchen. She had not
given dinner a thought and nothing was thawed. At least
he had bought enough eggs.

That proved he was all right. No man who thought to
buy eggs for himself and his family, who mowed the lawn
and put away all the dishes, would be capable of those terrible things. Why did she even think it?

She prepared a salad and a sauce for Spanish omelet.
As soon as he came home, she would cook the eggs.

A light meal for a hot evening. But not enough for a
big man. She set a pan of rice to boil.

A big man. Physically capable of—

But even a small man could overpower those girls. The
oldest, Toni Lemich, had been petite, they said. And small
men could be wiry. Foster Farand . . .

Her brain went round and round, so that she did not
hear his car until he slammed the door. She jumped, dripping egg from the wire whisk onto the counter. He was
coming toward the kitchen door, his jacket over his arm,
top shirt button undone. His face was damp with sweat.

"Hi," she said inadequately, and did not attempt to kiss
him.

"Have a good trip?" he asked.

"It wasn't exactly a pleasure trip, but it was good to see
the family again. I really should keep in touch more."

He glanced at the eggs, and she apologized. "We got
home too late to shop, and I forgot to thaw anything."

"That's okay." At least he was in a fairly good mood.

"Carl—why didn't you tell me?"

He stopped on his way into the living room. "Tell you what?"

"About the murder. Why didn't you tell me? On Monday night."

"Oh . . . I don't know. It was way over on the other side of town."

"But Cedarville isn't a big town. It's still the same thing. You said nothing happened."

"I said that? I don't know. Guess I wasn't thinking."

"You must have known. It was in Tuesday's *Post,* and I talked to you Tuesday night. You told me to look at the newspapers."

"That was another conversation, as I recall. What am I being grilled for, anyway?"

She had begun with a dry mouth, afraid to talk of it, but she was no longer afraid. Only confused. He, always so fascinated by the murders, suddenly sounded as if he had forgotten.

Was it real? Or an act?

"May I be excused to go and change now?" he asked.

"Of course. I didn't mean to keep you. I—just wondered."

During dinner, Mary Ellen chattered about their trip. Most of the talk seemed to be meant for her father. Hurtfully. She bubbled about Pennsylvania, making it clear that she had had a wonderful time and had been most reluctant to leave.

"I really don't see," said Joyce, "that Cork is any better than Cedarville as a place to live and have fun."

"It's much better," Mary Ellen insisted. "It's more countryish when you get out in the country. It's not so slick as here, and the village is nice and small-townish, with the pizza place and that store where you used to buy cosmetics." She leaned forward, resting her folded arms on the table. "And there aren't any *murders.*"

Joyce flinched, and dared not look at Carl.

"We have pizza parlors here, too," she said lamely, "and a variety store."

"It's not the same. Cedarville's like I said, it's too slick."

"I think I see what you mean. The people in Cork have less money, it's more rundown."

"I like it that way. It's homey. It's real."

So that, thought Joyce as she sopped up the last of her omelet, was what really appealed to Mary Ellen. It was not the down-at-the-heels atmosphere of Cork, it was the hominess. The solidity. And it was not a physical solidity that Mary Ellen missed, in the form of a single, steady home, it was something less tangible.

Later in the evening her curiosity overcame her and she went back to the newspapers for a more thorough look at the story.

Leslie Moore, the paper said, had been visiting a friend, and had evidently tried to thumb her way home. No one saw the car that picked her up. No one saw her again until early Tuesday morning, when a truck driver spotted her body in a patch of weeds and bushes near the road.

Also on Tuesday morning, a letter arrived by mail at the offices of the New York *Post*.

They thought they had me. I'll give them something to think about. Not that I care one f___ about clearing the wrong man, I only feel you ought to know the real slasher is not so stupid as to get caught. Certainly not so stupid as to confess. I'm pulling off another one soon, right under the snouts of the p-i-g-s, so watch for me.

Leslie Moore, smiling up from a family snapshot.

Chief of Police Francis D'Amico, asked to comment on the letter, said of course it was written by the killer. It'd have to have been mailed before the thing happened.

And how had the killer gotten away with it?

Nobody knew. The village and state police had been watching everywhere they could, and so had the half-formed civilian patrol groups. It was a hell of a thing.

She could imagine what Frank must be thinking about girls who hitchhiked. Of course he couldn't say it. Not about the dead. And now he would be blamed, despite his many warnings.

With a warm smile, Carl sat down on the arm of the sofa and looked at the paper over her shoulder. He nodded toward the picture of the girl, whose blond hair kept its sheen even on newsprint, and whose wide-set eyes looked up from under her lashes.

"Quite a little cockteaser, isn't she?"

For a moment the words did not register. Then they exploded in her ear.

The room shimmered with a kind of blackness that seemed to last for hours. When it cleared, her hand, holding the paper, had not moved, and Carl still stared bemusedly at the picture.

She closed the paper and threw it onto the table. She felt him look at her, but she could not face him.

Never, never again.

She got up from the sofa.

"Where are you going?" he asked.

"It's been a long day." She went upstairs, wishing she did not have to sleep in that bed.

She did not know when he came up after her. She was awake, but did not look at the clock. It seemed as though she had been lying there for years.

He puttered in the dark, taking his pajamas from a hook on the closet door. Then he left the room, and after a while she could hear the shower running.

He had already taken a shower when he came home. Shower after shower. He did perspire a lot.

She was still awake when he came later and got into bed beside her. With a conscious effort, she made her muscles relax. She could feel him watching her. He was lying on his side so that he faced her, and he watched. She remained motionless and tried to breathe evenly, but he knew she was not asleep.

The bed heaved as he stirred. He was up on his elbow now, bending over her. She shrank from his hands. This she had wanted for so many months, but now she shrank from it.

His fingers dug into her soft waist. He pulled her over onto her back. Then his hand was on her breast, under her nightgown. She squeezed her eyes closed, but knew she must respond. If not, he might be angered. She loosened her arm to reach up to him, but then he was on top of her and she could not move.

20

Friday was another steamy morning. She had never known a hot spell to go on so long, not with this kind of heat and humidity.

Again Adam fussed and fretted. She put him back in his crib after the early morning feeding. "I have no time for you now, Adam. I have to fix Daddy's breakfast."

Carl was in the bathroom, shaving. This early rising had become a routine even before Adam's birth. It was all a part of living in the country.

Later they sat at the breakfast table, she in her seersucker housecoat, he dressed, except for his suit jacket, which he would not wear until he boarded the air-conditioned train.

She watched him stir his coffee, and remembered Frank D'Amico stirring coffee. She must close her mind to Frank D'Amico.

Did she really know this man? Even sitting at the breakfast table, she felt oddly alone.

"Do you know what you did last night?" she asked.

"What did I do?"

"You raped me."

For a moment the look in his blue eyes frightened her. Then she realized that it was only alarm at her words, and not anger.

"Is that what you call it?"

"Well, yes. It was kind of savage."

"Did I hurt you?"

Was he sorry? "Yes, you did."

"I didn't mean to." His hand brushed hers. "It's been such a long time. It just came over me. Didn't mean to hurt you."

"I know, honey. It's been an awfully long time, but—"

134

"You call everybody 'honey,' don't you?"

She took her hands from the table and clasped them on her lap. "I'm sorry I'm so trite. I just can't call people 'darling,' it doesn't come naturally."

"Nothing to get excited about," he said mildly. She had not thought she was excited. "Darling" reminded her of Larry and his show business friends.

"Carl, what did you mean last night—what you said about that girl?"

He set down his coffee cup and looked at her, puzzled. "What girl?"

"In the newspaper. The girl who was killed. You said—"

He shrugged, and resumed eating. "I don't know what I said. Why? Never heard of the girl. Why would I say anything?"

Why would he? But he had.

Did he really not remember? Had he meant anything by it? Perhaps she was making a big thing over nothing. She felt some of the tightness slip from her heart.

It was nothing. Maybe he didn't even know she was the murdered girl.

"Your vacation starts Monday, right?" she asked, to make conversation. To get back to normal.

He nodded, intent upon buttering a piece of toast. She watched him, and wished that she could love him. She wished nothing had ever changed, that they could be where they had started.

He finished the toast and pushed back his chair. "Got to get cracking. I'll miss my train."

She had cleared the table by the time he came downstairs with his briefcase.

"About last night. I'm sorry if I hurt you." He gave her a quick kiss and walked briskly out to his car. She closed the garage door after him and waved as he drove off. His own hand flashed briefly in the car window.

She went back to the kitchen and found Gail sitting at the table. As usual, Gail had waited until he was gone.

"Mommy, what are we doing today?"

"We're doing laundry," said Joyce. "Won't that be fun?"

"I want to go somewhere."

"We've just been somewhere, honey. Now I have to catch up at home."

She wondered if she called everyone "honey" because her mother did.

"Why do you always have to be working?" Gail asked.

"Because that's life, and I'm glad you noticed I'm always working. Do you think I enjoy it? I'd give anything just to sit down and read a fun book."

"If we stayed in the apartment, you wouldn't have to do so much housework. It was smaller."

"It was smaller, but dirtier, because of the soot and dust. And I had to take the laundry out to the corner. That was a pain. A lot of my work is Adam," which Gail well knew, "but he'll grow up someday. That's just life," she said again.

When the kitchen was cleared, the beds made, the living room dusted, and the bathroom finally vacated by Mary Ellen who sometimes spent hours making herself beautiful, she was able to sort all the laundry that had accumulated on their trip and at home. While the first load washed, she had time to give Adam his bath, most of it, and leave him in Mary Ellen's care before returning to the basement.

The washing machine was still spinning. It was nearly finished, and she waited, leaning her elbows on the dryer.

She found herself staring at the floor, and wondered how long she had been staring. Had Carl scrubbed it? Who had scrubbed it? She had meant to do it herself sometime. Never got to it. A woman's work was never done.

Clean floor. Clean and shining laundry machines.

But clean only in this one place, over here by the laundry.

Who would have scrubbed this part of the floor, and why? Carl would have finished the whole job. He wouldn't leave half a floor.

She needed to sit down. There was nothing to sit on except the stairs. She huddled on the third step, drawing her knees close to her body and resting her cheek on them.

Nothing wrong with a clean floor. But why didn't he do all of it?

What's the matter with me?

She kept trying to think of reasons. He had spilled something. Bleach, maybe, and that was why it looked brighter. But Carl would not be so careless. He'd have put the cap on tight.

Raising her head, she noticed that the pile of newspapers on his work table had grown higher, and suddenly she knew they were not for recycling.

It was a while before she could make herself get up and look at them. The washer stopped spinning and waited for her. She turned on a light, and stealthily, as though he might be watching, lifted the neatly aligned edges of the papers. It was hardly a surprise that the pile began with the ones he had brought from the village that Saturday nearly three weeks ago, after the first murder was discovered.

Why shouldn't he collect a file of newspapers? He had followed the story since its beginning. It had happened right near his home, and his wife had been the one to report the first body. Why shouldn't he spill bleach on the floor like anyone else?

Through the open door she could hear Adam's voice, not crying yet, only fussing, but getting louder and more insistent. And Mary Ellen trying to soothe him.

The top newspaper in the pile. Frank D'Amico quoted as saying, "There's a nut running loose out there. People are scared."

And Mary Ellen at the top of the stairs with Adam in her arms. "He's hungry. Do you want me to feed him his applesauce?"

"I'll be there in a minute." Joyce reached up to switch off the light.

"What's the matter?"

"Just a minute, I have to put in the next load."

What am I going to do? She took out the damp sheets and undershirts and stuffed them into the dryer. She set the washer for a cold rinse, all the clothes from their trip, and pressed in the dial. *What am I going to do?*

Mary Ellen followed her around the kitchen as she plugged in the electric food-warming dish and opened a jar of applesauce. "Is something bothering you, Joyce?"

"Nothing. It's just the heat. It makes me dizzy."

Call Frank D'Amico? And tell him her husband collected newspapers and spilled bleach on the floor?

She wanted to talk to Frank. Hear his voice. She wouldn't feel so alone.

Mechanically she spooned the applesauce into Adam's waiting mouth. Of course there had only been that one night, when he said he had gone to the movies, and maybe he had.

No, there was the other time, when Toni Lemich—

She tried to think of a night when there had been a murder and he was safe at home.

The first one . . .

The newspaper said May 29. She was in the hospital then. She had just given birth to Adam, the night Joan Danner disappeared. He had been with her in the hospital, and left sometime in the evening, around eight, when visiting hours were over.

She did not know whether he had gone straight home.

And Valerie Cruz. That, too, had happened before they knew there had been any murders. She remembered reading about the girl's disappearance in the village weekly.

Last Monday night, it had said. She could almost see the print, although at the time it had not meant anything to her, except that it made her think of Gail, and she could feel the other mother's anguish. The girl had gone out on an errand. She lived in the village and the store was only a block away.

And Carl—he went out to buy ice that night, because it was hot and he wanted something cold after dinner, which meant a drink, and they had run out of ice, and the old refrigerator that came with the house took almost twenty-four hours to freeze a tray of ice cubes.

And he hadn't been able to find any, he said, it was all gone from the stores, which was why he took so long, and he was sweating.

And then Toni Lemich. He had worked late. He said he saw her get off the train, and he offered her a ride. He *said* she refused.

That was the night Mary Ellen was out, and she was terrified for Mary Ellen, but more because of what Carl would say, than that anything would really happen to Mary Ellen, because she could not believe those things were really happening right here in Cedarville.

But Mary Ellen would have been safe.

No, no, it wasn't true. Mary Ellen—no.

She wiped the excess applesauce from Adam's face. He had eaten well, been very patient with her. Carl's child.

Poor little baby. He hadn't done anything except get born, and—

No, it wasn't true. He *had* worked late, *had* wanted ice.

But why had Toni Lemich gotten off the same train?

She carried Adam upstairs to nurse him. To that bed where she slept beside her husband.

She sat down and unbuttoned her blouse. It was always a comfortable time, just the two of them. Adam and herself. She could read, or drowse. She tried to relax.

Turning her head, she could see the meadow with its bright daisies, and those purple things on stalks. The apple tree that had so enchanted Gail when it bloomed. She had wanted all this for her children.

And she would have it. She would make it all right again. *Stop thinking. It isn't true.*

21

It's not true. Not true.

It had been a crazy idea, and she was long since over it by the time Carl came home in the evening to start his vacation.

And yet, it had to be somebody. She wondered again what it would be like for the family of that person. When would they start suspecting? How would they know?

On Saturday he was up as usual to drive into the village. When he came back, he brought the papers into the kitchen and looked through them quickly.

"Nothing in there." He dropped them onto a chair and dug into the egg she set before him.

After breakfast he went out to mow the lawn. It was the same as always. She supposed he had mowed the lawn last Saturday, too, when she was in Pennsylvania. Of course it was the same as always. He wouldn't bother with it if—

Functioning on two levels.

When he finished and came in to take his shower, Mary Ellen was seated at the table wearing a Japanese kimono, her dark hair tousled and streaming about her face.

"Honestly, Daddy, do you have to make all that noise? A person can't even sleep around here."

His eyes raked over her, betraying him, and seeing nothing damning. The kimono covered her well.

"It seems to me you've slept enough," he said coldly, and went on upstairs.

Like any other father and daughter, Joyce thought as she emptied out the coffee grounds.

But she had seen the look in his eyes. He had stripped Mary Ellen naked.

"Is he going to be around all the time from now on?" Mary Ellen asked gloomily.

140

"For three weeks," said Joyce. "It would be nice if we could go somewhere, but we haven't the money, and you know how awkward it is, traveling with a baby."

"It wasn't so bad going to Pennsylvania. I could take care of Adam. You can pretend I'm the nursemaid. Let's all go to Florida. Cape Cod? Well, let's do something. If I were older," she continued, at Joyce's bleak response, "you could leave us all here with me in charge, and you and Daddy could go off somewhere. Wouldn't that be fun? Would you ever do that?"

"Not with a murderer running around loose," Joyce replied. She hadn't thought of saying that, but it comforted her. It put the murderer outside.

Where, of course, he was. There could be no doubt about that.

During the night she lay awake, dreading that Carl might approach her again. It had been so brutal the other time.

He didn't, but by morning, she was exhausted, and was not sure what had really kept her from sleeping. She dozed after feeding Adam, and when she went downstairs, Carl was on the sofa, engrossed in the newspapers. He told her they had recapped the story because it was Sunday, although there was nothing new to report.

"I can't understand why you're so fascinated by that," she ventured. "It has nothing to do with you."

He scoffed, "That's ridiculous. If people confined their interest to things that only had to do with themselves, there'd be nothing in the world. No arts, no science. We'd all be cavemen."

"Then where does this fit in?" she asked. "It's not art or science, it's just morbid. Why don't you want to read about the Middle East, or China?"

"I do. I read everything. And I notice you've been avoiding the papers. I can't help thinking there must be something wrong, if you have to make such a point of turning your back on this thing."

"There is something wrong." She stared down at her fingernails and waited for him to ask her what she meant, but all she heard was the crackle of paper as he turned a page.

Adam's schedule unbalanced everyone else's, causing dinner to be late that night. It was eight-thirty by the time they sat down at the table. They had scarcely begun to eat when the telephone rang.

Mary Ellen went to answer it. She remained in the darkened kitchen, and Joyce could hear occasional low tones and now and then a laugh.

Carl looked up from his dinner. "What's that girl doing?"

"Talking on the phone, I imagine," Joyce replied. "Maybe it's Barbara. She's been away, you know."

He hadn't known and he didn't care. He listened for a moment, frowning, and then called, "Mary Ellen!"

She appeared in the kitchen doorway, still holding the phone, and motioned that she would be there momentarily.

He called her again, louder. She put her hand over the receiver and squeaked "Okay! Okay!" A hurried good-bye into the telephone and then she came back to the table, gleaming.

"Who the hell was that?" Carl demanded.

The gleam vanished. "Somebody."

"I asked who it was."

"What difference does it make?"

"It makes a big difference," he explained without much patience. "You walk away in the middle of dinner, which is exceedingly rude, and you—"

"Can I help it if somebody calls in the middle of dinner?"

Joyce said gently, "You could always tell them you'll call back. I'm awfully sorry dinner's so late tonight."

"I want to know who it was," Carl repeated.

"A friend of mine, okay?" More than annoyance crept into Mary Ellen's voice. She was growing desperate.

He reached out and seized her wrist. "*I asked you who it was.*"

"Daddy!" She tried to pull away, but was no match for his large hands. He tightened his grip.

"Daddy, you're hurting me!" Tears came into her eyes. Gail turned away, sickened by the scene.

Rattling the slender arm, he shouted, "It was a boy, wasn't it?"

"How—how do you know?"

He rose to his feet and towered over her. His huge paw swung back and then smashed into her face.

Gail was the one who shrieked, fled upstairs and slammed her bedroom door. Mary Ellen sat crumpled in her chair.

Was she dead? Her neck snapped? Joyce reached out to touch her face. Slowly Carl sat down, apparently purged of whatever the phone call had done to him.

Mary Ellen was not dead. Joyce half lifted her from the chair and led her toward the stairs. Over her shoulder she said to Carl, "Thank you for ruining dinner."

She sat in the darkness on the rocking chair in their bedroom, after Mary Ellen had gone to sleep. It was the only thing the girl had felt like doing. Perhaps it was a retreat. Or she had been injured. Joyce had wanted to take her to a doctor, not only for Mary Ellen's sake, but to bring the problem with Carl to a head. Mary Ellen had refused.

"I'm okay," she had said, "but *he's* not. My mother always thought there was something wrong with him. She was afraid to let me come here, but then he said he'd get a lawyer because it's in the settlement."

If Barbara had known, she ought to have done something. Even if it meant hassling with the law, perhaps she could have proved that he was unfit. They might even have been able to make him get help.

Not that it would have done any good. He'd have talked his way out of it.

Perhaps Mary Ellen was a little young for romance, but to half kill her? It had been David, she confided later to Joyce, the boy who took her riding on his motorcycle. He had been away on a trip with his family and had come back only that evening. A perfectly innocent boy, even if Mary Ellen was a bit young. Perhaps only the adult mind would turn it into a romance.

What am I going to do?

She heard him coming up the stairs. Which door would he open? His footsteps stopped outside her own. Light from the hallway spread onto the rug. It was his room, too.

"All right," he said, appearing only as a silhouette against the light, "I put away the food that the rest of you were too silly to eat, cleared up everything, and started the dishwasher."

Adam stirred at the sound of his father's loud voice.

She tried to open her mouth, supposing that he expected to be thanked. Was he trying to make amends? Or trying only to show how normal he was, still functioning while everyone else fell apart?

The words that came out were not thanks. "I suppose you realize you overreacted," she said.

"I did?" He came on into the room. Now he was illuminated, looking frigidly down at her.

"If you don't realize it, you should," Joyce told him. "I think it comes from something way back."

That night he had babbled about the whore and the tits, he had mentioned boys, too. She could not remember . . .

He said, "I think you'd better leave that sort of thing to the experts."

"That's what I'm talking about. I mean for your sake. You'd be happier if—"

"Who's talking about happy?" he retorted. "I'm perfectly happy. You seem to be the one who's not. You see all sorts of smoke where there isn't any fire. Maybe you should go and get your head examined, since it's obvious that's what you're babbling about." He turned abruptly and left the room.

He hadn't closed the door, but she was still in darkness, over in her corner.

Was she wrong? No, that was part of it. They always denied it.

People who are physically ill, she thought in despair, want to get well. Why does this have to be different?

She remembered Dr. Ballard and his "Catch me, catch me." It was supposed to be a cry for help, but Carl didn't want any help. Or if he did, he wanted to be caught like a rodeo steer, roped and thrown to the ground.

Mary Ellen.

He loves her. He loves his daughter. People love their children. But Mary Ellen makes him angry.

People's children make them angry sometimes.

When did it start? When Adam was born. A male child. A threat? And the second one—when summer began and he knew Mary Ellen would come. And then those blowups over her clothes. It was not her clothes, it was Mary Ellen herself. How could Barbara have let her come?

She got up from her chair and looked out into the hallway. She *had* heard him go downstairs. Sitting on the edge of the bed, she listened, then picked up the telephone and listened once more.

She dialed Barbara's number and heard it ring. Again and again. Still gone. How long a vacation? She had to get Mary Ellen out of the house.

Her heart was beating so that she could feel it. She put the receiver back where it belonged.

What do I do now?

Call Frank? Dr. Ballard?

His footsteps on the stairs again. She ran back to the chair, so he would not know she had left it.

Got to do something.

"Are you going to bed already?" she asked when he entered the room.

"Nope. What are you sitting here for?"

"I'm thinking."

"About?"

"Just thinking."

There was something ominous in his voice as he asked, "Are you keeping secrets from me?"

"You've kept a lot of secrets from me." As soon as she said it, she was frightened.

Don't turn on the light, don't look at me.

"What do you mean I've kept secrets from you?" He moved toward the light switch, but stopped.

"All the things that go on in your mind." Even that was too much. She retreated. "So you can't expect to know everything that goes on in my mind. People need some privacy."

He opened the closet door and took his pajamas from their hook. Then he went into the bathroom and turned on the shower. But he wouldn't go to bed yet, because he could sleep late tomorrow. He would be around all day for the next three weeks.

*Got to get Mary Ellen out of here. That's the first thing.
But where?*

And even with Mary Ellen gone, there was still Gail.

And Adam.

And herself.

22

She wanted to spend the night in the living room with Adam beside her. But that would have left the girls upstairs—with him. And so she lay sleepless on one thin edge of the double bed, feeling his heat and his breathing.

All night she tried to plan what she would do. She could drive into town, ostensibly for groceries, and stop and see Frank D'Amico. But she couldn't leave the children, she would have to take them with her. And what if Carl decided to go, too?

Or telephone, if he would ever leave the house. She should have called Saturday while he was mowing the lawn. But Saturday she hadn't known.

And maybe she didn't know now. Maybe she was wrong. She had no proof. Only his violence with Mary Ellen, and the times he was out. And the clean basement floor.

It was enough.

But what if it wasn't true? What if she told them, and then it wasn't true?

Finally the room began to lighten, and Adam kicked and made small waking noises.

She slid out of bed without waking Carl. Perhaps he would get up early and drive into the village for a newspaper. She carried Adam downstairs and sat on the living room couch, watching the picture window while he nursed. There was no one to see her. No killer out there.

Maybe there is. Oh, please, God.

A killer. *Out there.* Her brain felt heavy from lack of sleep.

After a while she heard him get up. Heard him go into the bathroom and turn on the shower. Adam finished feeding. She went back upstairs and lay on her bed, trying to sleep. She heard the shower go off and then the buzz of his electric razor. He came out of the bathroom fully dressed.

"Go ahead with breakfast," she told him. "I feel rotten."

She would call someone as soon as he drove off to buy the paper. But he didn't go. He came back upstairs bringing her a glass of orange juice. She could never call. He would come into the room at any moment.

"Coffee?" he asked.

"Okay." It might help to wake her up.

He brought a steaming cup, with just the right amount of milk. Why was he being so solicitous? To throw her off the track?

Maybe I'm paranoid. Maybe he's right. *I'm* the one who needs help.

After a short sleep she felt better, and got up and dressed. She wondered if he had gone for the paper while she slept. He hadn't. She tried to think of something else he could buy at the drugstore where the papers were sold. Some reason to send him there. Baby powder? Diapers? She had everything, and he knew it.

And then suddenly the car keys were in his hand. "Want anything?" he asked.

Her mouth opened. "A melon."

"A what?"

"A melon. For breakfast tomorrow." She hadn't even thought of it, the words just came. It would send him to the supermarket, prolong his stay in the village. "And a half gallon of milk."

"We have milk."

"I know, but the kids use a lot of it on their cereal. And bananas. Adam's supposed to eat mashed bananas. Do you want me to write it down?"

He said he could remember it. She tried to think of something in another department. "Baby cereal," she called after him. "Rice flavor."

He was gone. She dialed the police station, and kept her eye on the driveway in case he came back for something. Not that Carl would, he was too organized.

Too organized. Of course he was not the one. An organized person would never—never do those things.

"Cedarville Police. Finneran."

"Oh—" It had rung, and she had forgotten. Brain still foggy. "Is Chief D'Amico there?"

"No, he's not. Can I help you?"

"No, I—" She could only tell it to Frank, not anyone else. They would come with their sirens screaming and their guns drawn, but Frank would understand. "Will he be there today?"

"He'll be in later. Want to leave a message?"

"Listen, this is terribly important. Is he home? Do you know where he is?"

"I can take a message. He'll call you as soon as he can."

Damn it, didn't they have radios in their cars? Didn't they carry walkie-talkies, like the New York police? She had forgotten that this was Cedarville. She left her name and phone number. It was all she could do.

She glanced at the daisy-shaped clock on the wall. He had been gone only five minutes. Would barely have reached the drugstore by now. It was still quite early, but that didn't matter. Psychiatrists got calls in the middle of the night. She looked him up in the Westchester phone book. There was only one Ronald K. Ballard, M.D.

A woman answered, "Doctor Ballard's office."

"Is he there?" she asked.

"No, dear, this is the answering service. Can I help you?"

Can you help me? Yes, you can all help me.

"Do you know when he'll be in?"

"Not till Thursday. Would you like another doctor? I can—"

"No, thank you." She hung up the phone. Huddling into a chair, she clenched her fingers like claws over her face. But then she heard Gail's bare feet padding down the stairs.

Gail came into the kitchen, wearing her thin seersucker pajamas. She looked around warily.

"He's gone to do some errands," Joyce told her.

"Mommy, I want to go back to the city."

She wanted to go back in time. Before Carl.

"We've no place to go in the city, angel."

"But I hate it here!"

"I know. I'll try to think of something."

"Why can't we go to Pennsylvania?"

Could she? Send Gail there? At least for now. Gail alone might not be too much for them. She was quiet, and would help if called upon.

"I could ask." And put her on a train, perhaps, or a bus. She could travel alone, if someone met her.

"Don't ask *him*."

"I didn't mean him. Listen, Gail, do you remember Chief D'Amico? The policeman who asked you those questions? He might be calling me later. If you answer the phone, just get hold of me quietly. Don't tell anyone else, okay?"

Gail's face seemed to sharpen and grow taut. How much did she understand? She was a city child, and knew what the police were for. And that infernal television taught children everything.

"I'll explain later," Joyce said, hoping to keep her from speculating too much. "Is Mary Ellen up yet? I wonder how she's feeling."

"I heard her radio."

After an hour Mary Ellen came down the stairs looking pale and haughty. She was fully dressed in a pair of dark blue shorts and the tee shirt with the CB lingo. No one could complain about her clothing that morning.

Her father, who had returned from the village and was sitting on the sofa reading a newspaper, looked up as she passed. She moved her eyes, took him in, and showed no flicker of expression as she glided into the kitchen.

So it's going to be like that, Joyce thought. At least she could stare him down. She's got the upper hand.

Mary Ellen selected a box of cold cereal and took her place at the table. The telephone rang. Joyce picked it up.

"Frank D'Amico. That you, Joyce?"

"Oh—yes."

She heard the paper rustle and then Carl stood in the doorway, watching her.

"You called me?" Frank prompted.

"Yes, I—" Her eyes met Carl's, and retreated.

"I'm sorry I bothered you," she said into the phone. "It wasn't really anything."

"I see. Are you sure you're all right?"

"I'm sure. Thank you."

Carl asked, "What was that all about?"

"Nothing. The operator." She sat down weakly in a chair. Why hadn't she handled it better? Somehow alerted Frank? Why hadn't she taken the children and fled while Carl was in the village?

The phone rang again. She snatched at it, but it was only Anita. "Hi, Mrs. Gil, can I talk to Gail?"

Bright, cheerful, and irritating. She called Gail, who answered upstairs. Mary Ellen wailed, "What's with this telephone? I've got a splitting headache, and it won't stop ringing."

Joyce looked at her sharply. "You have a headache?"

"And a stiff neck. I took a couple of aspirin."

"I'm not surprised." It was the shock. The jarring effect.

After the aspirin began to work, Mary Ellen felt well enough to help with Adam's bath. She would not have missed it for anything, she said.

"And I like feeding him, too," she told Joyce, "he's so cute and messy. I wish I could nurse him the way you do."

"Good God, don't let your father hear that. But, Mary Ellen, I was thinking— The way your father's behaving, I was wondering if it mightn't be better, when your mother comes home—"

"Oh, I can stand him," Mary Ellen said airily. "Except for last night. That was a little too much."

How to explain?

Mary Ellen would not leave—in truth she had no place to go until Barbara returned—but Gail wanted badly to get out of the house. While Mary Ellen fed Adam his mashed bananas, Joyce secluded herself in the bedroom and put through a call to Pennsylvania. Her mother should have been home, but when she realized it was already noon, she was not surprised that no one answered. Mom would be at the hospital, or on her way there.

Carl appeared in the doorway, just as she set down the receiver.

"Who was that?" he asked, with the very faint smile and the calmly cheerful tone he so often used.

"I was trying to call my mother."

"What do you want to call your mother for? You just saw her."

"I wanted to find out how Dad's doing."

"Wouldn't it make more sense to wait until evening when the rates are lower?"

Yes, it would. Also Mom would be home then. She shrugged and said distantly, "It just came over me. I'm really worried."

He turned his head and listened, hearing a new voice downstairs. "Who's that?"

"Anita. She called a while ago. Probably wants to play with Gail's dolls."

He left the bedroom just as Mary Ellen came in with Adam. Again the cold exchange of looks, but his went farther than her face. Joyce noticed it, and Mary Ellen did, too. There was a sudden hardness about her.

She's only here, Joyce realized, because her mother trusts me. And I can't seem to do anything.

23

Anita noticed the closed bedroom door. "Is your mother sleeping?"

"She's feeding the baby," Gail said. Already Anita was getting on her nerves. She would not even have agreed to let her come over, except that Anita was so insistent.

"Then we can go," Anita said.

"Go where?"

Anita wandered into Mary Ellen's room and turned on the small red radio. Mary Ellen swooped to grab it away from her. "You messed up my favorite station."

"I'm sorry," Anita said huffily, and turned her attention to Gail. "We have to go back to that place and get my peacock. I mean Denise's peacock, and the horse. I really have to get them."

Gail shook her head. "I'm not going back."

"You have to. It's partly your fault I left them there. If I don't get those animals, Denise is going to kill me."

"It's not my fault," Gail argued. "You stole them. And I'm not going back. That's where—"

Mary Ellen looked up from readjusting the radio. "Why do you suddenly need them now? They've been there for ages. It was the day before I came."

"Because Denise is going to kill me," Anita repeated. "I told her I'd get them back this afternoon. I—"

"Why can't you just buy her some new ones?" Mary Ellen suggested.

"She'd know the difference. Those come from a Japanese store near my father's office in the city. You can't get them here. Anyway, she doesn't know where they are. I told her—" Even Anita seemed embarrassed by the monstrousness of her statement. "I told her you had

153

them." She suppressed her uneasiness and fluttered her eyelashes at Gail. "I told her you borrowed them."

"Well, you can just un-tell her," Mary Ellen said as she put her radio back on the dresser. "You have no right to tell lies about Gail."

Anita chose to ignore her. "Please, Gail?"

"They're probably gone by now anyway," Mary Ellen continued. "There've been police and searchers all over the place."

"I'm talking to Gail, in case you didn't notice."

"All right, Gail can do what she wants. But I think you're a turd."

Gail looked out of the window at the bright steamy day. It was like that other day, the last time she had seen her cave-rock. She would never forget the smell of that thing under the leaves.

Of course you couldn't smell it from the cave-rock and anyway it was gone now, for a long time.

Maybe if she only went as far as the cave-rock, and only for a minute. She, too, had worried about those beautiful animals staying out there to be rained and snowed upon, and broken.

She wouldn't tell Mary Ellen, who would only think she was being a jellyfish. She drifted out of the room and down the stairs, looking to see if Carl was anywhere around, so she could avoid him.

Anita danced beside her and seized her hand. "Are you going with me?"

"Only for a minute," Gail said. "Just to see if they're still there. And after this you'd better not take any more things that aren't yours." With Anita in her debt right now, Gail could safely lecture her.

At the foot of the stairs she stopped to fasten on her shoes, and then they went out into a day just like that other day.

"Watch out for Mr. Lattimer," Anita warned as they climbed through the stone wall. "Aren't you scared, with him so close to your house?"

It had not occurred to Gail to be afraid of him. He was so stiff and shuffling and self-contained, she had never thought of him as much more than a rather pungent part of the scenery.

"Do you think he killed those people?" she asked.

"I know so. My mother said he did."

"Then why don't they arrest him?" Gail glanced nervously at the roof. There was no smoke rising today. Perhaps even Mr. Lattimer had realized that he did not need a fire in this weather.

"Because they haven't got anything on him." Anita knew that kind of language from her cousin, who was a policeman. "But they're watching him," she added. "They found some clothes and stuff in one of those buildings on his place."

Gail felt a lurch somewhere in her middle. If she had known about that, she would definitely have been afraid.

She looked back at the apple tree, for she had been too distracted to check it as they passed. Even the growing apples were spoiled for her now, with home so unbearable because of Carl. And Mr. Lattimer.

They climbed over the other stone wall and down the slope to the brook. She tried to see up toward the beginning of the brook, which was somewhere on Mr. Lattimer's place, where the police had found those clothes. It was lost in the leaves. Everything was lost in the leaves down here. You could hide. She slapped a mosquito on her arm. You could hide in these green leaves. Maybe he was hiding here now.

Then up the hill through the jungle of white stalks. They were like bones, those stalks.

As the woods opened around her, she felt a quickening. She did not know whether it was eagerness to see the cave-rock again, or fear. She pushed it from her mind.

"They're here!" cried Anita, running up the hill ahead of her. "They're still here! Gail, there's junk all over this place, and the people don't have any clothes."

She sat down to clean off her animals, which had gotten dirt in their tiny grooves. Gail surveyed the garden. Leaves and debris had fallen out of the trees, and the moss was littered with cigarette buts, a flip top, and a cellophane wrapper. The pebbles that had neatly lined the moss beds were scattered and some of the moss uprooted.

"Who did that?" Gail demanded.

"Those police and other people." Anita picked up the trash and threw it over the side of the hill. Gail crouched down and began to straighten the pebbles and replant the moss. She didn't care so much about the people. They could always make more of those, but the garden had been her masterpiece.

"Where's the queen?" Anita scratched about under the rock. "We'll never find another dress like that for the queen."

"It doesn't matter." Gail patted the moss back into place. She wished it would rain. That might help it along. "Maybe I can find a piece of lace. Or foil, that would be nice."

"Maybe we could bring your dolls out here."

"No, they're too big."

"The palm tree's gone. I'm going to pick some more leaves. They never got to have their party that night." Anita reached up to the branches that overhung the cave-rock and removed a few leaves. She began to dress the stick figures. Gail thought of going down to the brook for water, but had nothing to carry it in. She found the twig that had been the queen, and looked for something new in which to dress her.

Their murmuring voices blended with the forest, and all the watcher could see through the leaves were splotches of white and yellow from their clothes, and the glint of Gail's blond hair.

He saw an arm reach out now and then, and their legs folded under them as they sat. He dared not move. In the woods, something would crackle. He could only watch those young limbs and hear their voices. A glaze covered his vision. He began to feel the dampness, and took out a cloth to wipe his face.

He forgot that he was growing cramped, waiting there. The glaze spread from his eyes to his whole body. He always liked it when this happened. He didn't feel like himself anymore, or even something that was made of flesh. He was protected and borne aloft.

The murmuring voices grew sharp. "Well, *I'm* going to put them over here. It's supposed to be a dance, not a sit-down party. You're no fun."

"You're no fun. You always want everything your own way. This was my cave-rock, and now you're trying to boss it around."

"It's both of our cave-rock. I brought the horse and the peacock, that's more than you did, so it's mostly mine."

"Then I'm not going to play anymore."

"Ha ha, you're just mad because it's mostly mine."

The flash of white and the blue shorts came into view more clearly now, scrambling down the side of the hill. He could have gone after her. It would have been logical.

He watched the long skinny legs and the blond hair hurrying down the path. If she hadn't been so angry, she might have seen him. She was disappearing now, over the hill toward the brook. He wondered if she would come back. Not likely. And if she did, he could see her from up there.

He turned his attention to the other one, sitting cross-legged among the rocks, humming to herself. He'd love to get hold of that hair, that little round body. She had no right to tease him like this. Or anyone. Again the dampness came, and again he wiped it away. It was all over him now, soaking his clothes. His hands started to tremble. That was the way it came on. He could feel it everywhere. He felt it in his groin.

Carefully he pushed aside the low branch just in front of him and took a step forward. His foot rustled in the leaves. He waited, but she did not look up. Still humming, she tossed her head and ran her fingers through her hair.

She had forgotten about Gail, until she heard someone coming.

But it wasn't Gail. "Oh, hi," she said.

He didn't answer. His eyes looked funny, and he shivered as if he was cold.

At the same time, he sweated all over his face and arms. She thought maybe he had gone a little crazy, the way he looked. She watched him, and felt swallowed up by those strange eyes.

She didn't think about being afraid until he was almost there. Then, when she drew in a breath, he was on top of her. She felt a sharp crack at the back of her head. She was down on the rocks looking up at the sky. His big hand squashed her mouth. She couldn't breathe.

A white thing gleamed and went into her mouth. Soft

and white, it filled her throat. She gagged, trying to force it out.

He flipped her over so her face was in the moss. A pebble bit her forehead. She couldn't move her legs, and when she tried to free her arms, they stuck together.

In a flash, she realized she was tied up like those girls. She tried to scream, to shake him off, but couldn't move.

She saw the rocks whirl about her, and the trees and sky as he rolled her onto her back. For an instant she saw his face, then squeezed her eyes shut. Wriggling and squirming, trying to fight her way free, she didn't even feel the pain in her arms that were tied beneath her.

He tugged at her shirt. A knife slashed and her chest was bare. Again she squirmed. The knife sawed and ripped at her shorts. She felt the air on her nakedness.

He pushed back her legs. He was too strong. She couldn't move. He thrust up inside her, burning and tearing. Then the big hands came down on her throat and the blackness roared in her head, bigger and bigger until it crushed her.

24

During the afternoon Joyce tried twice more to call Frank D'Amico. He was out, they said. Out most of the day. She did not leave a message, nor did she want to speak to anyone else. She trusted Frank.

When the telephone rang at five o'clock, she dared hope he was trying to reach her. Perhaps he had gotten a hidden message from what she said before.

It was Sheila, asking about Anita.

"She was here earlier," said Joyce, "a couple of hours ago, but I think she left." The house was quiet, except for Mary Ellen's radio. "She must have started home."

"*Started* home? A couple of hours ago?"

"I really don't know when she left, I've been busy. Maybe she stopped off somewhere."

She heard Carl come in the front door and his heavy tread go straight upstairs.

"Okay," said Sheila. "If you see her, tell her to come right home."

He must have been working outside. She could hear the shower running. She hadn't seen him anywhere out there. In this heat, you would need a shower after just taking a walk.

It was time to think about dinner. Would it be like last night? Probably Gail wouldn't even come to the table. Maybe not Mary Ellen, either.

That reminded her of her plan for Gail. She tried again to call Pennsylvania, listening all the time in case he turned off the shower.

"Mom?" How could she explain? "Mom, listen, I know you're busy— How's Dad, by the way?"

Dad was getting better. Still in the hospital. She told her mother that Gail was upset over the murders. "It's extra bad because she remembers about Larry. She can't even go outside to play."

Naturally her mother was worried about *her,* if it was that bad. Joyce said it was not like that, it was only Gail. If she could just get away for a while . . .

As she had known, her mother could not refuse. She sounded quite pleased about it. Joyce would make reservations and then let them know when Gail was arriving.

She felt almost lighthearted as she hung up the phone. That was one thing solved, even if only for the time being.

A car came up the driveway. A black one, the Farands'. As she went out to meet it, she looked for two heads in the front seat and saw only one.

Sheila leaned from the window. "I've just driven all the way from my house to your house and she's nowhere along the road. When did you say she left?"

The pounding feeling again. She was afraid Sheila might see it.

"I really don't know." It was true. "I had all these things to do, and I just wasn't concentrating." But she thought it had been some time ago. Quite a long, long time ago. Maybe with Gail. But Gail had come back.

"Look, Sheila, I'll watch for her. Why don't you go back along the road? If she stopped anywhere, you might have missed her. And I'll ask Gail."

Sheila hesitated. Probably she wanted to ask Gail herself.

Joyce urged her again. "She must be somewhere along the way, since she already left here."

Hours ago.

Sheila would notice how upset she was. Her frantic smile. "I know how you must feel," she added.

Sheila nodded and turned on the engine. "You'll let me know?"

"Of course." But Sheila would find her. She *would* find her.

The shower was still running as she hurried upstairs. He always wanted to be terribly clean—after yard work.

"Gail?"

Gail looked up from *The Wizard of Oz.*

"Gail, where did **Anita go** after you left each other? Do you know?"

Gail's lips parted as though trying to frame an answer.

"She didn't go anywhere. We were at the cave-rock. She got too bossy, so I came home."

"The cave-rock?"

"That place. We just went— She had to get something. And then we fixed up the garden, but—"

"*You went to that place? The fairy palace?*"

"I didn't mean to, but she said—"

Without waiting for Gail's explanation, she ran down the stairs. He was still in the shower, thank God.

Still there. What would he do when he came out?

Run all the way. Of course there wouldn't be anything, it was all in her mind, there wouldn't be anything, he was only doing yard work.

But there might be someone else. Mr. Lattimer. What if he came? She could pick up a rock.

Down over the brook and up through the dead white stalks. Like that other time. But she had walked that time.

She walked when she reached the foot of the hill. She couldn't see anything. Don't let there be anything.

Two cautious steps up the hill.

Her breath stopped. For a moment she was not really sure. Perhaps only because she expected it.

But it *was* there. It was real.

The gaping red. She saw red everywhere. The face.

She got as far as the brook, and then sat down among the white stalks.

Go home. It was her sanctuary. She had automatically started for home.

She couldn't go to the Farands'. It was closer, but she couldn't.

She didn't want to see them.

Her children. With *him*. She made herself stand up. Her feet began to move, but she felt nothing in her legs. None of it was real. She floated.

The screen door grated on its spring and she stopped to listen. Upstairs the water was still running. She must have been gone only a second. All that in one instant, like a dream.

She looked in the kitchen. Empty. Chopped meat thawing on the counter. Had she done that?

She picked up the phone.

"Police." It was Finneran again. The young Finneran that Mary Ellen had liked.

"Up here . . . In the woods . . . Where you found the first body, the next hill."

She hung up. Something about the shower bothered her. He couldn't be in it that long.

She looked out of the kitchen door, and then the picture window as she passed it on her way upstairs. She didn't see anyone, but something was all around her. She could feel it.

Very slowly she tested the bathroom door.

It opened.

Through the shower curtain—no one. The water poured cold, chilling the room. She started to back away.

His hand closed over her wrist. She felt his body like a wall against her back.

His blue shirt. She could see the sleeve. He was dressed, except for shoes. He still wore his rubber thonged slippers. For an instant she caught the scent of soap on his skin. In that instant everything was all right. Then he twisted her arm in back of her. The other arm, too, and something tightened around her wrists.

She whimpered, "Carl?"

He guided her into the bedroom where Adam lay kicking. Adam would be hungry soon. Her breasts felt heavy with milk.

He pushed her across the bed. Her head fell toward Adam. She remembered that gaping red thing in the woods and tried to kick her way free.

"Carl, the baby—"

He knelt across her legs, tying her feet.

She screamed. Mary Ellen— Gail—

"Where are they?" Through tears, just in time to see the door close.

Her screaming made Adam start to cry.

"Adam . . . honey . . ." Would he know her voice? She could roll over, sit up, but could not get free.

She tried to think. A pair of scissors for cutting hair was in the top drawer of the dresser, across the room. He had used clothesline rope, she could see it on her ankles. It would take years to cut through that with barber's shears.

Adam paused, gasping for breath. Far away she thought she heard a scream, quickly muffled.

Mary Ellen's radio playing.

"Mary Ellen!"

The baby-lamb cries began again. A helpless sound. She struggled across the bed.

What would he do with them? That gaping red thing.

Anita.

If I'd done something sooner.

But I didn't *know*.

The door opened. She had half sat up to reach the baby. Carl pushed her down and cut the bonds from her feet. Now—

"I didn't believe it," she told him. "I just didn't believe it."

He dragged her to her feet, so that she faced him. He held a gun. She had never seen one up close, like that, pointing at her.

"Where are your car keys?" he asked.

"My—what?"

"Car keys!" He seized her arm and shook her.

She nodded toward her purse on the dresser. For a happy instant she thought he was going to take her car and drive away.

He nudged her toward the dresser. "Get it."

"I can't. My hands—"

"Turn around."

She felt cold metal against her wrists and the bonds fell away. When she turned back, he was still pointing the gun at her.

He jerked his chin toward the purse. She picked it up. He prodded her toward the door.

"What about Adam?" she asked. He prodded her further.

Maybe the gun wasn't loaded.

She dared not take a chance. He could overpower her even without it.

"What are you going to do?"

He pushed her toward the stairs. "Get in the car and drive."

Behind her, Adam screamed for his mother.

"Where's Gail?" she asked, and stumbled on a step. He caught her. "Where's Mary Ellen?"

They were not in their rooms. She should have looked in the basement. Oh, God, that clean basement floor. That poor young girl with the shiny hair.

"Carl, you can get help," she pleaded. "They'll know you need help, they won't blame you."

The gun pressed into her back.

When they passed the front door, he stopped to lock it.

"Carl," she said, "Adam's upstairs alone."

He pushed her into the kitchen. After they went out through the back door, he locked that, too. He nudged her toward her car.

"You just can't leave the baby here alone," she cried. "Where are the girls? Carl, where are the girls?"

"We're going to be all right," he said. "Get in the car."

She halted. "Not until you tell me where the girls are."

"If you don't get in the car," he informed her pleasantly, "you'll never find out where the girls are."

He opened the door on the passenger's side and ordered her in. So he could slide in after her without ever taking the gun off her.

She turned the key. "Where are we going?"

"Just start driving. Head for the city. I'll tell you."

She looked back at the house as she swung around and started down the driveway. At least the windows were open, but they all had screens that hooked from inside. Would anyone be determined enough to cut through a screen or break down a door? Would anyone know Adam was there, would anyone care? Would they even think of it?

They won't know we're gone, she thought. Nobody can see the house.

The girls were dead. There had been no sound, except that scream, and she was not even sure she had heard it.

They were in the basement. Dead.

He asked, "How much gas do you have?"

She glanced at the gauge. "About half." And the car was economical.

"Carl, really. This isn't going to help you."

"I'll be the one to decide." He sounded so calm, so rational.

Down Shadowbrook Road. She wished they would pass another car, anybody who would see them driving away together. Damn, she hadn't given her name to the police.

It wouldn't have done any good. Even if they were stopped, he would use her as a shield. He wasn't going to give up. Not Carl.

"You can't go on like this," she said. "You can't run away forever, and you can't run away from yourself."

"Forget it."

Where was Gail? She had been so afraid. And she might have gotten away, maybe even tomorrow. If only—

And Adam. Little Adam. He had only just been born. Wouldn't somebody—

"Carl, you can't do this!"

"Keep driving."

Right through the heart of Cedarville.

"Turn left," he said. It was the road they took to Paradise Lake. "Get on the Taconic."

Not through Cedarville. No one would see them. No one on the Taconic Parkway would care.

"Do you know," she began, "I want you to save yourself, because I love you."

The words caught in her throat. She hated him.

"We had a good thing going, Carl. We can have it again. You can get help."

"I don't need help," he said through clenched teeth.

Damn the bitch. He could see through her. She hated him.

It wouldn't be long now. He only needed her to get away.

He looked down at his feet. Those rubber thongs. Hadn't had time to change. They had to get out of there before somebody came. Before she suffocated.

He wondered how it would be, walking through the airport in rubber thongs. Perhaps they would see, and stare at him.

He could feel the eyes. Like that other time.

"Better not," he said. "Those eyes."

He felt the car jerk as she started to slow it. Then she kept going. "What eyes?" she asked.

"They stared at me. All those eyes."

"When was that?"

"You wouldn't know." She disgusted him. She was not Daniella. Even Daniella didn't know much. Hadn't cared.

"Her old man beat me up," he said. It had hurt. All he'd wanted was to touch the girl. Just touch her. He needed a girl and Daniella hadn't cared. She went off strutting her tits and wagging her ass at the boys. She never cared about him. She left him, and Mama, too.

"He hurt. My face. All beat up, see?"

She was watching the road. He said, *"Look at my face."*

"I can't, Carl, I'm driving."

"I said look at my face."

She looked at him quickly and then back at the road.

She loved him once. Mama did, too, and Daniella. Even the girl. They all loved him. He never had to ask, they just loved him.

But then they beat him up, and Mama had to get him out of town. Out of the state, even. She said he'd never have a record because he was a juvenile, and she'd fix it up anyway. She said she knew he didn't do it.

But the other people stared. He remembered coming out, his face hurting, and all those eyes.

"They asked if I wanted a doctor."

Again she turned quickly and glanced at him. "A doctor could do a lot for you," she said.

"A lot of bullshit. It doesn't hurt now anyway. That was twenty years ago."

"I don't mean— I mean— They could help you live with yourself."

"Go to hell. I already live with myself."

"Yes, but they could help you with—"

"God damn it, stop trying to pretend there's something wrong with me! You're crazy. That's what you are, and you know what they do to crazy people?" He raised the gun that had been resting on his knee.

He saw her face tighten. They were almost at the Taconic Parkway now. He would have to decide about the airport.

25

They had taken the body away, but it would be a long time before the blood was washed from those rocks and the mangled moss grew back.

Frank D'Amico cursed himself. He knew he wasn't the only one cursing him. It *had* to be someone around here. At this point, he guessed he could write off Foster Farand, and even Bruce Cheskill and the Gilwood guy. They were all commuters, and they hadn't been home when it happened.

What a thing for Foster to come home to.

He saw Herb Mackey standing a little way off, staring at the moss.

"She was a relative of yours, wasn't she?"

Herb nodded.

Frank rested his hand on the other man's shoulder. "What can I tell you?"

It was his fault. He was in charge, he should have come up with something. People had screamed when he released that lush from New York. But he knew it wasn't right. It didn't solve anything to hold the wrong man, just to satisfy the bloodlust that was growing in this town.

At Hawthorne, Carl ordered her onto the Saw Mill River Parkway. She remembered driving there last fall when the trees were red and orange. A family outing. The four of them, for she had just learned that Adam was on the way. Carl had been normal then. Or had he?

Peaceful Westchester. The sun shining through the trees. People exercising their dogs on the grass beside the Saw Mill River, which was really just a brook.

Her breasts were starting to hurt. And if she hurt, what about Adam?

How had she gotten herself into this? They gave him a blood test when she married him. That was all she knew. His *blood* was okay, for god's sake. What about the rest of him?

He must have a plan. Carl was too intelligent to blunder into the city without a reason. She had a plan, too. There'd be people, and traffic lights. She'd run through a traffic light and then there would be that blessed sound of a siren . . .

"Stay on the right," he said. "Take the Cross County Parkway."

"Where are we going?"

"Stay on the right."

She almost didn't see the exit to the Cross County Parkway. She wondered how long her nerves could hold out. He told her to keep to the right, keep bearing right. The parkway widened and entrance ramps merged on the right. She had to watch for cars on those merges, and he was in the way, and he wouldn't help her. He would not take his eyes off her for one instant.

"Thruway south," he said.

A sharp turn to the right. For a minute they were on a local street, with a traffic light, gas stations, and a line of cars. *Please, God.*

And then on the Thruway, which soon became the Major Deegan Expressway. They were in New York City now. In the Bronx. A diesel truck roared past them. Then another. The noise tore her to pieces.

"Where?" she asked.

"Just keep going to the Triborough Bridge."

The Triborough was a toll bridge. She would have to stop and hand them some money. Wouldn't they see that gun on his knee? Couldn't anybody see it?

26

In Cedarville, the neighbors clustered around the Farands' house, but there was nothing anyone could do.

Nothing Sheila could do. She was helpless and boiling. There had to be something.

"Why can't they get him?" she demanded of Pamela Cheskill, who had brewed a pot of coffee—as if that could make any difference.

"Don't you want to lie down?" Pamela asked. "Maybe the doctor could give you something."

"No, I don't want to lie down." Sheila slapped away the hand that tried to comfort her.

Foster had come home an hour ago. They couldn't reach him before, because he was on the train when they found Anita. She wondered how "they" knew. An anonymous phone call, they had said.

"Why can't they get him?" she asked again.

"Who do you mean, dear? Foster? He's with the police. Don't you remember?"

"Don't be so dumb." Sheila stood up, brushing past her friend. She had no friends now. Only a stone where her heart used to be.

"I don't mean Foster, I mean *him*. That depraved pervert out there. Why couldn't they get him before—"

"They've been trying."

"What do you mean trying? *I* could have told them. All those people getting killed, and he's running around free. They should have locked him up the first time. Right there in the woods, his whole playground, he had the whole place to kill little girls."

She ended, choking, wishing she could cry. The cold stone wouldn't let her cry.

169

Pam's green eyes seemed to swim before her. "Who do you mean? You don't mean Lattimer?"

"Who the hell do you think I mean? He's a killer. Maybe he'll start on boys. Maybe he'll kill Brucie."

She saw Bruce Cheskill jerk up his head. Bruce Cheskill needed a daughter, then he'd care.

"They're going to leave him there," she screamed.

"I'm not going to leave him there!" roared Bruce. She did not know what happened, but suddenly he had a rifle in his hand. He must have gone next door. She must be having blank spells and he had gone next door. It was all crazy, like a dream, but she knew it wasn't going to end like a dream. It would go on and on for the rest of her life, with Anita dead.

"Let's go," Bruce called. They murmured and shuffled. What was wrong with these people? Sheila heard herself speak. "Do you want another kid to get killed? How many kids do you want dead, you bastards?"

Somebody said something about the police.

"Oh, go to hell." Tears suddenly ran down her cheeks. "They had a whole month. A whole month and five people dead."

"*I'm* going." Bruce charged through the door. Sheila's own daughter June was suddenly there, her eyes red and wet, and then Denise. And the Massey boys from down the road, and some of the others.

Pam called out, "Don't kill anybody, will you?"

They followed the path Anita had walked so many times to go out to the woods, or over to Gail's house. When they reached the little hill, she turned away and wouldn't look at it until they were past, and then she had to look, but couldn't see anything. Not even any policemen. She wondered if they were already there, at Lattimer's, taking him in. Where the hell were they?

At the brook they turned northward along a less trampled path, probably the one he used to come down and kill her baby. There was the springhouse where Herb said they found the scraps of cloth. God damn, they could have taken him then, there had only been two deaths, and Anita would still be alive. Nothing they could do would make her alive anymore, it was incredible the way it happened so fast and then nothing could change it ever again.

"Shut up, you people, he'll hear us coming," she said.

"Him hear anything?" laughed one of the Massey boys.

"All the better," said Bruce. "He'll know what it's all about."

Excitement rippled through her as they approached his house. She watched for his face to peer out of a window and suddenly become transformed with terror, but there was no face. Was he too drunk even to know? Damn him, he was going to know.

Things still seemed to be happening in blank spells. Now she couldn't remember any of the walk over. She saw Bruce march across the front porch and burst through the door. She ran to catch up.

Bruce stood still. They were all still. The house seemed dead, hot and stuffy, and there was a smell.

And then she saw him lying by the cold fireplace next to a wooden table that crawled with insects.

Footsteps clunked over the porch and Herb came in. "What are you all doing here?"

"Oh, Herb." She sagged against his chest, a stupidly feminine gesture.

Gently he stood her back on her feet. "Out," he told them. "Out."

"But—" she couldn't seem to understand what had happened.

"Okay, you came to get him and he's dead." They obeyed like sheep as Herb ushered them back over the porch. "We already checked that. We sent for an ambulance."

"Who killed him?" she demanded.

"Nobody. You can see, he fell and hit his head on the table. Been dead a couple of days."

"Are you sure?"

They all looked at each other. Her eyes turned to Bruce. But he'd been in the city. What about the Massey boys?

"Herb," she said, "who called the police?"

"About Anita? I don't know. Some woman."

"A *woman?*"

"Didn't leave a name."

"What did she say?"

The others gathered close. Herb tried to remember what

the report had been. "She said it was near where we found the first body. The next hill, she said."

Sheila's head began to spin. She wondered if she was going to faint. She had never fainted in her life.

The next hill. Who knew exactly where they had found the first body? Who saw it?

Who was the person—? Who—this afternoon—had been so nervous when she came in the car, looking for Anita? Who had tried to get her out of there fast, *alone*, instead of going with her to ask Gail where they had been playing? Instead of helping her, as any friend would, to find her child?

"God damn," she said slowly. It didn't tell them anything, but it was all she could think of.

"You know who that woman was? It was Joyce Gilwood."

"How do you know?" asked Herb.

"Because I God damn *know*."

"We've been checking everybody around here. They're not home. The house is locked."

"Of course they're not home, you dumb cop."

She began to walk alone down the path beside the brook. Anita's brook, where she used to play. At first she was not sure what was going to happen. Everything seemed to be just happening, without her doing anything or even deciding anything. She reached into the pocket of her denim skirt—Pamela had helped her put on a skirt because it seemed more dignified than shorts—and felt a matchbook there. She had known the matchbook was there but did not have any distinct recollection of putting it there, nor any conscious plan for it.

All this time, she thought. All this time it wasn't Lattimer at all.

She looked back and realized that they were going with her. She had almost blanked out again, almost forgotten all about them.

She clutched the matchbook tightly, as though squeezing the fingers of someone who would help her.

Adam, Joyce cried to herself. Little Adam, alone. How could he do that to his child?

They looped around Kennedy Airport. She waited for

him to tell her which exit to take, which terminal, but he said nothing. There had been traffic jams on the Van Wyck Expressway. With the cars and trucks closing in she had waited for someone to notice the gun, but nothing happened.

"Carl," she said again, "which airline do you want?"

Around once more. You had another chance if you missed your terminal.

"Don't be stupid," he told her.

Sometime they would run out of gas. She wanted it to happen right there, where he couldn't do anything. She wanted him to get on a plane. Allegheny? Delta? Aero Mexico? She didn't care.

The sun was going down in a blaze of golden clouds. How could it be so late?

Golden clouds and golden rays. She had always thought that was heaven up there. Anita was in heaven. And Gail. She could have gone to Pennsylvania. Gail could have been safe.

"Forget it!" he barked, as though she had spoken before. Was she losing her mind?

"Forget what?" her nerves were shot. Mustn't speak crossly and upset him.

"Get out of here."

"Out of—the car?"

He gestured furiously at a sign that pointed back to the Van Wyck Expressway.

Out of the airport was all he meant.

It wouldn't work, he decided. There were too many complications in taking a plane. They'd wonder why he didn't have luggage. And with *her*. She was wearing shorts. And barefooted. He should have made her dress better. There hadn't been time.

"You'll take the Whitestone Bridge," he said, "and the Hutchinson River Parkway."

That was a good idea, the Hutchinson. They wouldn't expect him to be on it.

He could be pretty sure there was something else they wouldn't expect. They wouldn't think he'd be going back toward Cedarville.

The Gilwood house was locked up tight, just as Herb had said. Sheila chewed on her lip. It was maddening. They shouldn't have gotten away.

She was further maddened when they came around to the side of the house and saw two police cars in the parking area and Frank D'Amico standing in the open door of one. Those mirrored sunglasses hid his face even though the sun had just gone down.

If he didn't have a gun, she would have killed him. He should have done something.

He raised his hands and waved to silence them, just the way he'd done at that meeting, with Joyce—her fingers tightened on the matchbook—with Joyce sitting right next to her.

"Okay, people, let's cool it." The bastard, as though he was talking to a bunch of kids.

The place was overrun with cops. She could kill every one with her bare hands, but the Gilwoods first.

Bruce Cheskill yelled, "Where are they?" He thought they were hiding in the house. She knew they were gone. Joyce's car was gone.

"Nobody's going in that house," said D'Amico. "I'll go in myself when I get a search warrant. But you won't find them here."

Bruce turned to the neighbors. "How does he know?"

"Her car's gone," said Sheila. Frank glanced at where the car was usually parked. He knew.

She backed away from the others, wishing she hadn't called attention to herself. They were impotent with all those cops there. They were defused, in spite of Bruce wanting to fire his rifle. They would be sent home, like kids, but she still had her matchbook, and no one was looking.

She backed farther away, until she found a basement window that was open just a crack. Right below it were those two upholstered chairs Joyce had wanted to get rid of, and next to them, the woodpile. She remembered how, in early spring, Carl had gone out in the woods with Foster and they'd cut up some fallen trees.

She lit a match and touched it to the other matches, and the whole book blazed up. She dropped it through the window.

"That's for Anita," she told the house.

Frank watched them start away. Jesus, a lynch mob, right here in Cedarville. Herb's cousin, too, but Herb had told him how they marched on Lattimer and found him dead, and then were coming here. Somehow the Farand woman knew it was Joyce who called the police.

He'd thought of that himself. He thought—too late. Everything was too late. He hadn't realized the guy was home this week. Thought he was in the city, but now it all fell into place. Too late.

She was gone. He didn't know where the kids were. He remembered how she'd been that night at the pizza parlor. Full of questions and jumpy as a cat. Had she suspected even then? Why hadn't she told him?

He couldn't blame her, really. You just don't believe a thing like that.

And now she was gone.

He'd already asked for a search warrant. Now he radioed for the number of the car. He didn't know whose name it was registered in, and gave both of them.

He listened and, far off, thought he heard a sound, like music. He couldn't be sure, there was too much noise, too many people around. Probably one of them carried a radio.

He looked up at the windows. If he thought there was anybody there, he'd bust his way in, but it looked empty.

He ordered the people away, back over the stone wall, the way they had come. Then he got in his car with Finneran and they drove back to headquarters to wait for the search warrant and, more importantly, the number of the car.

Gail heard them leaving. Their voices and all that noise faded away. She heard everything so clearly, but she hadn't been able to make them hear her.

He had thrown her into that thing they said was a coal bin. She had always been afraid of it, a dark, black hole, probably full of spiders. Now she was in it. Every now and then she felt something crawl across her, and she screamed and shook herself, but she couldn't scream loud with the gag in her mouth, and she could hardly move.

Her hands were tied to her feet. The ropes cut into her and she was doubled up in a painful position, and had been for ages, but she couldn't get free.

At first she had thought her mother would come. For a long time she had been so sure. Now she wasn't sure anymore. They had all gone away and left her. The house was quiet, except for a faraway sound like water going through the pipes, and Mary Ellen's radio which she could hear sometimes, a note or two when it played loud. A couple of times she even thought she heard Adam crying, but now there was nothing, and it was probably her imagination. They wouldn't go off and leave Adam.

Only her.

But then the people had come. She didn't know why or who they were. She thought they might be looking for her, and made all the noise she could. She even heard a man say, "What's that? Hear it?" and another replied, "I don't hear anything."

And now there was starting to be a smell, like smoke. It was like when they had the fireplace in winter. They sat in front of it, she and her mother, and she could almost pretend Carl wasn't there.

Except this wasn't winter. And the fireplace was upstairs, but she could smell the smoke down here.

27

They were back in the country now. Joyce was not sure where, in the dark. It was one of those winding roads between Cedarville and Croton. They didn't even have names, as far as she could tell, although she supposed they must. Where did he think he was going?

The gas tank read empty. She knew it would run for a while even after it reached the empty mark. And if they ran out in these backwoods, he would probably shoot her and start walking. She was so tired she might not even care.

Except for Adam. And if Gail was still alive.

"Pull over there," he said.

Pull over? She saw a clearing off the road, sort of a dirt ramp that led into the bushes.

"Watch it," he told her as she nosed down the ramp. The earth dropped off just beyond it.

"Out."

He opened the door and made her slide over to his side. He would shoot her now. Her legs were stiff and they nearly buckled when she first stepped onto the ground.

Then he made her get back in, turn off the headlights, remove the trunk key from the set in the ignition, and take a flashlight from the glove compartment. And then they went to the back of the car.

"What are we doing here?" she asked.

"Shut up."

He told her to stand where he could keep an eye on her. He held out his hand for the key, and unlocked the trunk.

The lid flew up. There was a body inside. She screamed. The body moved and let out a moan.

"My God, Mary Ellen, are you alive?"

177

Carl took something out of the trunk and slammed the lid.

Joyce grabbed for the lock. "Carl, she'll die!"

He stopped her with the gun muzzle in her belly. She couldn't have opened it anyway, he had pocketed the key. He handed her a wrench and a large screwdriver and told her to remove the license plates.

She knelt in the dirt and began to struggle with a corroded nut and bolt. Mary Ellen was here and Gail dead. A penance for her not being sure, not speaking. For Anita's death. He had left her in the basement at home.

Mary Ellen had been tied and gagged and in that trunk for a good three hours. How could she breathe?

He kept the flashlight shielded, the gun against her neck, and told her to hurry. What if she couldn't get it off? She knew now what he planned to do.

"Carl, it's almost out of gas."

He didn't bother to answer. With the new plates, he would never be spotted. And Vermont plates at that. Where had he gotten them?

She was ready to try anything. Leave the bolts loose and hope the plates would fall off, and someone would stop the car. He noticed what she was doing and made her tighten them.

She stood up. The plate was secure.

Got to get Mary Ellen out of there. Get the key somehow.

"Carl, let her out. She'll die in there."

Tantalizingly he tossed the key and caught it, dropped it back into his pocket. He motioned her to the front of the car.

"The front plate," he said. "And speed it up."

Through the trees she caught a glimmer of light. Could she run out onto the road?

He would shoot her if she tried. But Frank had said—*run.*

He was standing over her with the gun. She crouched and loosened the bolts that held the plate. The bushes concealed her, and the car ran past and was gone.

Finally she was able to straighten up. Her knees barely held her. She slipped the tools into her pocket.

"Go over there"—he pointed to where the earth

dropped off beyond where they were parked—"and throw those plates over."

It was not as deep as she had thought. Down at the bottom she could see the glimmer of beer cans and paper, the outline of an old tire. She tossed the plates, heard them crash, and turned to go back.

His arm was raised, pointing the gun at her head.

She screamed.

RUN, Frank had said. There was no place to run. Bushes everywhere. Only back up the slope.

Her scream, her sudden dodge, caught him off guard. A shot exploded and missed. She veered, and suddenly—

Into the car.

Thank God he had left the ignition key. The wheels spun on loose gravel. He lunged at the door beside her. She snapped the lock.

He raised the gun. The car lurched forward and a back window shattered.

She caught the flash of his shirt and then his face before her. He was on the hood.

She couldn't see.

He grinned at her. He lay sprawled across the hood, clutching a wiper and pointing the gun at her face. She couldn't see the road.

Lights. She turned on the lights. Now she could see a little.

She couldn't stop the car, couldn't get out, not with him there. Get Mary Ellen out. Get him off.

28

"We got the license number, Frank."

"Get out an APB."

He didn't have much hope. They'd have ditched the car by now. At least, if it were found, he could tell which direction they were going. Maybe.

The car? He'd have ditched them all. The guy couldn't travel with a wife and kids.

He felt like a jerk, sitting around the station. Nothing he could do.

"I'm going back up there."

He suddenly saw them all, maybe upstairs in a bedroom or down in the basement. He saw her with blood in her hair, lying on the floor.

He was in his car, at the wheel, not thinking. Finneran slid in on the other side. "Want me to drive?"

Frank started the car. If she had blood in her hair, a few seconds wouldn't make any difference, but he wanted to drive.

"Watch for that number," he said. Not that it would be anywhere around here.

They were up the hill in maybe two minutes.

"Jesus," he yelped when he saw the house.

Finneran grabbed the radio and called the fire department. It was a small, volunteer department. It'd take forever.

How did this happen? If Gilwood had done it, it would have burned hours ago.

Unless he came back.

No time to force the doors. There was an open basement window, but that was where the fire was. Two chairs and a woodpile. Jesus. He reached in to close the window, hoping to cut off some air, and then he heard the screams.

She was driving toward Cedarville. In town, they'd see him.

She felt as if she was going about eighty miles an hour. Twice the car skidded onto the shoulder. Couldn't see. If someone came— Please, someone.

The road to Cedarville . . .

He jerked his gun arm, pointing urgently. Another road. Not the one to Cedarville.

She started to turn.

He was going to kill her anyway. She spun the wheel back. The car swerved. He slipped, and grabbed tighter to the wiper.

She lost all fear. She was cool, calm. He had slipped. He pointed the gun at her eyes.

She swerved again. Zigzagged across the road. He clung to the wiper but couldn't aim the gun.

And then he vanished.

She couldn't believe it. A trick.

The wiper was gone.

She pressed the gas pedal. The road danced before her. Adam. And home. She would go home.

Little Adam upstairs.

Suddenly the steering wheel flew out of her hand. She saw trees ahead, and fought to control the car.

She slammed the brake. It barely slowed. Dear God, power steering and power brakes and out of gas. She pumped the brake, held with all her strength to the wheel, but she hadn't any strength. The trees hurtled toward her.

She felt the crash and waited for worse. Nothing came. The car was off the road, the headlights smashed, but the underbrush had acted as a cushion.

Her leg hurt and there was blood where the screwdriver in her pocket had stabbed her. It woke her up. She snatched the key from the ignition, forced open the door, and ran to the trunk.

The key. He had taken the trunk key. She tried the one she had. It jammed in the lock and she couldn't get it out.

The screwdriver was a big one, half an inch thick. She pried at the lock, bent the metal of the lid, but the lock would not break.

She looked back, hearing a sound. How far had she come before the crash? Did he still have his gun?

She wrenched again at the lid. Finally she ripped the metal so it tore away from the lock.

"Mary Ellen!"

The girl whimpered. Her hands and feet were tied, her mouth gagged. The bonds on her feet were clumsily wrapped, probably after he had thrown her in there.

She heard the sound again. Like running footsteps. She tugged at the bonds on Mary Ellen's feet. They were clumsy but strong, and it was too dark to see.

"You'll have to try— I can't carry you."

Ridiculous to think anyone could run like that. At least she could pull the gag off Mary Ellen's mouth.

As soon as it was off, Mary Ellen began to choke and cry.

"Oh, Joyce . . . my own father . . . it makes me sick. I'm going to be sick."

"Sshh, I think he's coming." She struggled with the rope, pulling, tugging. One strand slackened, another tightened. Mary Ellen cried out. She pulled still tighter and at last worked a loop over the bare feet.

The rest of the rope slid off. She helped Mary Ellen from the trunk. She would have to guide her. The girl was stiff from her hours of confinement. It would be hard to run with her hands still tied, and with her tender bare feet.

Now she heard the footsteps clearly. He was coming around the bend, running heavily, his whole body bent forward. He lifted his arm. He still had the gun.

"*Run*, Mary Ellen."

How far to Cedarville? It was miles. Maybe three. More than they could run, the way they were. She heard his feet, a heavy *slap, slap*. The rubber thongs.

"*Run*," she said to Mary Ellen. "Run!" Their only hope: their feet. He had a gun. And longer legs.

"Joyce, there's a house. Joyce." Mary Ellen doubled over, holding her side. "I'm going to die."

She could see it through the trees. The lights. They couldn't draw him to the house.

"You go," she said. "I'll keep on the road. Don't let him see you."

"No."

Only twelve years old. She was afraid to go alone.

"Mary Ellen, we have to, there's no other way. If we

both go, he'll get us both. Tell them to call the police, Cedarville police." She pushed Mary Ellen up the short driveway, and as she ran on, watched her darting through the shadows.

Please be good to her. At least they would believe her. They'd see her hands.

Too late she realized that Carl might assume they had both gone to the house. She couldn't see him now, there had been another bend. If she went back, she would waste precious time.

But she couldn't let him get Mary Ellen.

She heard his *slap, slap.* Heard him stop. She could see the house lights, but no longer the driveway. Or him.

She picked up a stone and threw it across the road.

"Get up, Mary Ellen," she said. "You've got to get up and *run.* Get *up.*"

She began to run again. She couldn't hear his feet for the sound of her own. She stopped. There was nothing.

Slowly, silently, she crept back until she could see him. He was standing at the end of the driveway, watching the house.

Carl, that was Carl. Her husband. And now a stranger. With a gun.

He didn't know she was there, watching him.

She picked up another stone and moved closer. Could she do it? Outside the house, a floodlight sprang on.

If she missed, he would know exactly what she was doing. And then he would have to choose—her or Mary Ellen.

She took another step, and lowered the stone. She couldn't. Not him. Not anyone, in spite of the gun.

She couldn't—but what about Mary Ellen? The people in the house, innocently involved? Just because she couldn't.

She swung back her arm and carefully aimed. Couldn't see him very well. Couldn't get closer. She aimed and threw the stone.

It sailed past his head and crashed into a bush at the foot of the driveway. She saw the blur of his face as he whirled around.

She ran into the underbrush at the side of the road. It

slowed her, but at least he couldn't see her. Couldn't see she was the only one. The bushes scraped and tore at her.

She saw him on the road, pointing the gun at her. She screamed as he fired.

She felt nothing. He had missed.

"Run, Mary Ellen," she called again. "You go that way. I'll—"

Another shot. And then moving lights. A car.

She stumbled from the bushes, waving her arms. The car veered to miss her and sped on. Unbelieving, she saw its taillights vanish around a bend. One unbelieving instant, and then Carl leaped from the bushes.

She ran, knowing no one would save her. No one cared. How many shots left? Just keep moving, and it was dark. Only the dark would help her. Run to Cedarville. Three miles.

Another car. Two. She turned her face to shield her eyes from the light.

Then it slowed, blazing in her face. It hurt. She didn't understand at first that it stopped. She heard a door open. Strong arms went around her and held her up.

"It's okay now," said Frank D'Amico's voice. "It's okay."

He started to help her into the car, then flung her against it as shots resounded in the woods.

She tried to see, but he blocked her, protecting her. There were voices, more shots, crashing of bushes.

Then someone said, "We got him, Chief. I think he's dead."

Frank turned back to her and held her tightly against his broad chest. "It's okay," he repeated. "It's all over now."

"Mary Ellen," she whimpered. "My children. My Gail."

29

She would not go back to the house. The fire was only a minor reason. They told her it smelled of smoke, but was not really damaged. It had smoldered in the chairs and then the woodpile. Probably a cigarette, Finneran allowed.

Frank nodded, and said nothing. She could see it on his face. It was no accident that a cigarette, or whatever, had gotten inside the house. She could hardly blame them, whoever had done it. But how did they know? How had they known it was Carl?

"I didn't know," she said again and again. She couldn't touch the sandwiches or coffee the police had sent for. Perhaps she would spend her whole life there, in that room in the police station. With Frank, and Gail and Adam, and Mary Ellen.

Mary Ellen couldn't stop crying, sickened by her father, by her ordeal in the trunk. She cried even for him, now that he was gone. And in the midst of her tears she ate three sandwiches, and Joyce knew she had a resilience that would carry her through.

Frank asked, "What are you going to do?" When she failed to answer, because she didn't know, he said, "I could put you up at my house for a while. You gotta stay somewhere. I think at this point we could all use some sleep."

And they would be safe with him.

"They'll get over it someday," he added. Meaning the mob. The fire. It seemed she could almost read his thoughts, and he hers.

"I wasn't sure," she said, "not even then. Not until he came up behind me at the bathroom door. Do you think they'll ever understand that?"

185

"Of course they will. Look what you went through, and your kids."

"It wasn't as bad as what happened to them. But I really didn't know." To her dismay, her voice broke and tears rolled down her cheeks.

Clumsily he patted her hand. She wished he would hold her, the way he had when he found her on the road. But maybe not here, in front of the children.

"Nobody's blaming you," he said.

"But I—I wondered. I just couldn't believe it. I wanted to ask you. And Dr. Ballard. But then it seemed so crazy."

"Mommy," said Gail, "can we go and live in Pennsylvania?"

She saw the look on his face. She knew Gail was right. They should start over again, in a different place.

"Yes, I suppose we can," she said, "for a while. Until we sort things out and decide what we really want to do."

Her eyes met Frank's. He would understand that, for now, at least, Cedarville was not the place for her. After tonight, he would help her get away. And then—

"Let's keep in touch," he said.

About the Author

Caroline Crane lives in New York City with her husband and their teenage son and daughter. She is the author of SUMMER GIRL, as well as of six books for young adults.

Ø

Bestsellers from SIGNET

☐ **THE INTRUDER by Brooke Leimas.** (#E9524—$2.50)*

☐ **THE SUMMER VISITORS by Brooke Leimas.**
(#J9247—$1.95)*

☐ **THE DOUBLE-CROSS CIRCUIT by Michael Dorland.**
(#J9065—$1.95)

☐ **THE ENIGMA by Michael Barak.** (#J8920—$1.95)*

☐ **THE NIGHT LETTER by Paul Spike.** (#E8947—$2.50)

☐ **ASTERISK DESTINY by Campbell Black.** (#E9246—$2.25)*

☐ **BRAINFIRE by Campbell Black.** (#E9481—$2.50)*

☐ **BLOOD RITES by Barry Nazarian.** (#E9208—$2.25)*

☐ **LABYRINTH by Eric MacKenzie-Lamb.** (#E9062—$2.25)*

☐ **UNHOLY CHILD by Catherine Breslin.** (#E9477—$3.50)

☐ **COLD HANDS by Joseph Pintauro.** (#E9482—$2.50)*

☐ **TULSA GOLD by Elroy Schwartz.** (#E9566—$2.75)*

☐ **THE UNICORN AFFAIR by James Fritzhand with Frank Glicksman.** (#E9605—$2.50)*

☐ **EDDIE MACON'S RUN by James McLendon.** (#E9518—$2.95)

* Price slightly higher in Canada

Buy them at your local bookstore or use this convenient coupon for ordering.

THE NEW AMERICAN LIBRARY, INC.,
P.O. Box 999, Bergenfield, New Jersey 07621

Please send me the SIGNET BOOKS I have checked above. I am enclosing
$_____(please add $1.00 to this order to cover postage and handling).
Send check or money order—no cash or C.O.D.'s. Prices and numbers are
subject to change without notice.

Name _____

Address _____

City _____ State _____ Zip Code _____
Allow 4-6 weeks for delivery.
This offer is subject to withdrawal without notice.